Found

the

crescent chronicles

ALYSSA ROSE IVY

Cover Design: Once Upon a Time Covers

Formatting: Polgarus Studio

ISBN-13: 978-1490591759
ISBN-10: 1490591753

OTHER BOOKS BY ALYSSA ROSE IVY

To the city of New Orleans, thanks for all the good times.

Acknowledgements

Thank you to everyone who believed in this series. I'm honored to have been able to share this story with you.

Special thanks to Grant for everything, and to my amazing children for making my days so much fun. Thank you to Kris Kendall for the stellar editing, Kristina Scheid for proofreading, and Stephanie Nelson of Once Upon a Time Covers for designing such an awesome cover. Thank you to Jessica Watterson for being a fantastic beta reader, and thank you to Jennifer Snyder for being the best author BFF I could ever dream of. Thank you to all of the bloggers who take the time to help me spread the word about my books. Thank you to my readers—you make this journey so much fun.

Chapter One

If Levi mentioned my sex life with Toby one more time I was going to slap him.

"I don't see how it changes anything. You already knew I wasn't a virgin."

"I thought you'd been with a human. That's different. Human men don't count. I assumed I was your first Pteron." The serious expression on his face made me want to laugh despite my anger.

"That's ridiculous." I tied the laces on my running shoes. I was antsy from spending so much time inside and was excited that Hailey was coming by Levi's house to meet me for a run.

"It was nothing like it is with us, right? Just tell me that."

I let out a deep breath. "How many human girls were you with before me?"

"Uh—"

"Yeah, I thought so. Does that mean what we have isn't special? Different?"

"Of course not." He sat down next to me, leaving no space between us. "Those girls meant nothing. You mean everything."

"Exactly." I decided not to berate him about the disrespectful way he treated women before me. "You may not have been my first Pteron, but you're my favorite." I kissed him on the cheek. I was trying to pretend it didn't weird me out, but I was going crazy. How was it possible for me to have been with two different Pterons? I wasn't even nineteen yet.

His shoulder brushed against mine. "Have we had sex more times than you guys did?"

"What?" I shot up and away from him. "No. No. No. We are not talking about this anymore. Say it again and you can forget about us having sex any time in the near future. Got it?"

He put up his hands in mock defense. "Fine. I just don't like it."

"You've made your feelings abundantly clear." I turned to walk out of his bedroom to wait for Hailey. I didn't make it through the doorway.

His arms wrapped around my waist and pulled me back against him. "How long do you have before Hailey gets here?" He kissed my earlobe before trailing a line of kisses down my neck.

"Not enough time." I spun out of his arms. "I wouldn't want to cut your amazing skills short."

He laughed. "Just wait until tonight, Al. I'll show you amazing."

"I can hardly wait." I leaned up and kissed him. I should have known it wouldn't be just a quick little kiss. He wasn't having any of that. He had me pinned against the wall within seconds. My hands were tangled in his hair almost as quickly.

That was exactly how Hailey found us. "I'd tell you to get a room, but I guess you already have one."

Levi reluctantly backed up. "Impeccable timing as always, Hailey."

She shrugged. "What can I say? I have the touch."

"That you do. Let's get out of here." I ran a finger down Levi's bare arm. "Don't get too bored without me."

"I probably will. See you girls later." He waved.

We stopped on the porch to stretch before taking off running down the block. We cut over to St. Charles Avenue to run the street car line. Hailey had to try hard to run slow enough for me to keep pace. If you want an inferiority complex, spend all of your time with paranormal creatures.

"Do you know what you're wearing tonight?" Hailey asked.

"I'm going to wear that red strapless dress I picked out with you a few months ago." We were going to a paranormal New Year's Eve party. I figured a short, sexy dress worked no matter what kind of party it was. I wasn't thrilled about going, considering how worried I was about Jess, but the deeper I could get into Society events, the better chance I had at finding out how to get her back.

Hailey laughed. "Trying to make Levi's night, huh?"

"Why not? Maybe it will make him shut his mouth about Toby."

"It's crazy though, isn't it?" She sped up again, forcing me to push myself harder to keep up.

I watched her red ponytail bobbing in front of me. "Definitely. I just wish I knew how it was possible. It can't be a coincidence."

"You think there's more to it? Like what, you're a Pteron magnet or something?"

"A Pteron magnet? Those exist?" I barely got the words out. I was already out of breath.

"Of course not." Hailey turned, running backwards. "I thought you've been training with the guys."

I stuck my tongue out at her. It was childish, but she deserved it. "Sorry, we aren't all as fast as you."

"I'm only running at half speed."

"Remind me again why we're friends?" I finally gave up. I stopped and bent over, clutching my knees.

"Because you love me." She stopped too.

"Do you love me enough to carry me home?"

"No, but he does."

I didn't need to turn around to know that Levi was behind us. "Normally I'd get mad at you for following us, but right now I don't care."

I turned and let him pull me into a hug—a sweaty hug. I was the only one who was sweaty. He was perfectly dry in his black running shirt and gray shorts. He always looked good in gym clothes.

"Do you really need me to carry you?" His tone was hopeful.

"It's tempting, but I'm going to keep going. Think you can walk next to me or something? That would probably be the right pace."

Hailey sighed. "I can try again. I really did try."

I smiled. "It's okay, Hail. Go on ahead."

"See you guys in a few." She disappeared down the street.

I gave myself another few seconds to recover. "Ready, favorite Pteron of mine?"

FOUND

"Always." Levi didn't actually walk, it was more like a jog. It probably took effort to go so slow, but he didn't seem to mind. I'd only been back from Vermont a few days, and I don't think he wanted to let me out of his sight. A week before it would have annoyed me. But after learning about Jess's kidnapping, I didn't mind the extra protection.

"Did Jared find out anything else?" With Bryant locked up in The Society equivalent of a prison, Jared had moved up the chain. Although he wouldn't be a full-fledged security officer until after graduation, he was in on all of the decision making.

"Not really. She's still being kept in that house, but she's unharmed. I promise you, she's going to be okay. If we thought otherwise, we'd go in and get her. It's just not worth tipping the Blackwells off about our inside man yet. We need to find out more before you and your friends are safe."

"Is Emmett still there?" The only thing keeping me remotely calm was finding out that Jess' boyfriend was with her.

"Yes. They're going to be okay."

"I hope so. I feel awful."

"Don't."

"You make it sound so easy. My best friend's been kidnapped because of me."

"We'll get her back, Al. I promise."

I tried to smile, but it wasn't easy. I knew she wasn't being hurt, but she was still being denied freedom. I also had no idea what would happen when Toby found out I wasn't going to him. What if he took it out on her?

"Ready to turn around, or do you want to keep going?" He gestured further down the street.

5

"Let's head back. Hailey wore me out."

He laughed. "Sounds good. Since you're so tired, you'll need my help in the shower."

"Your willingness to help astounds me sometimes."

He grinned. "It's so good to have you home."

"You do realize I'm moving back into my dorm when it opens, right?"

"We'll see." There was a twinkle in his eye that let me know he wasn't buying it.

I let it go. I was sure we'd have plenty of time to argue about it later.

Chapter Two

"Maybe you're right. We should stay home." Levi's eyes devoured me when I walked out into the living room.

"No way. I just went through all this effort to get ready. We're going." I gestured to my hair and makeup.

Hailey told me that everyone in the New Orleans shifter community would be at this party, and that tons of shifters from around the city would come in for it. I didn't know how I'd use the night to find out more information, but I was determined to try.

"We can just go a little late." He took a step toward me. I couldn't really blame his reaction. I was wearing a short dress in his favorite color—red. I'd left my hair wavy, which took just as much work as straightening it did, and I put on slightly more makeup than usual. A pair of three inch stilettos finished off the outfit. Levi might tell me he loved my eyes, but my legs were his weakness. A short dress and high heels would have him eating out of my hand. I wasn't being mean. I'd be coming home with him at the end of the night.

"Looking good, Allie." Jared whistled when he walked out of his room. Like Levi, Jared was dressed in a tailored black suit. If I had to guess, they were both Armani.

Levi glared at him. "Watch it, Jared."

I laughed. "You aren't actually threatened by Jared, are you?"

"No. I just don't appreciate my best friend checking out my mate."

"Then tell her not to wear something so sexy." Jared snagged his keys off the counter. He loved pushing Levi's buttons.

"Okay, let's get this over with. I have no interest in sleeping with Jared. Okay?" I put a hand on Levi's arm. His eyes looked dangerously close to turning. He seriously needed to calm down with his insane jealousy.

Levi put a hand under my chin to make me look up at him. "I know. This has nothing to do with a lack of trust. I just don't like anyone looking at you that way."

"I can change…"

He moved his hand to my cheek. "No. That won't be necessary."

"Good." I slipped on a black wool peacoat. New Orleans had warm winters, but it was still cold in late December. "So Hailey says this party is at the Eiffel Society. That's the crazy looking place on St. Charles, right?"

"Crazy looking? You mean cool? The building was actually part of the original Eiffel Tower."

"As in the one in Paris?"

"What other one would I be talking about? My family had it brought over in the 1980s. We aren't the ones on record for the deal, but you know how it is."

"How it is?" I suppressed a smile. Sometimes Levi forgot I didn't grow up in the same world he did.

"Yeah. My grandparents are pretty connected to our French roots." He rarely talked about his grandparents. The only other family outside of his parents I'd met was a quasi-crazy cousin who burned down a frat house to either kill or threaten me. I never did find out which.

"So other than the building, what can I expect?"

"Craziness. Expect craziness." Owen joined us. He was dressed in a black suit as well. It was the first time I saw any resemblance to Hailey in him. Maybe it was the way his light skin looked against the black. Hailey had really pale skin too.

"I'm here. The fun can start." Hailey walked in, tossing her coat on the back of the couch. She was dressed in a short, purple halter dress. Her hair fell in tendrils around her face, and she looked incredible.

"Did Dad see you leave the house in that?" Owen eyed his sister skeptically. Since the dorms were still closed, she was back at home. She was planning to spend the night on the guys' couch.

"I was wearing my coat."

"Please don't do anything stupid tonight." Owen scowled. "I don't want to have to beat up some idiot for you."

"I am more than capable of taking care of myself, but it won't be an issue. Who's going to bother me? The only one I plan to dance with is Allie. That is, if Levi gives me the chance."

Levi had his arms wrapped around me. "I'm not making any promises. I don't plan to let her out of my sight dressed this way."

Hailey laughed. "Like you would let her out of your sight tonight even if she were wearing oversized sweats."

"Very true. Like Owen said, it's going to be crazy." Levi leaned in to me. "You are going to be one of the only humans there. Do not go anywhere without one of us. Scratch that, anywhere without me."

"You're not coming to the bathroom with me."

"Okay, that you can do with Hailey. But no other exceptions." There was nothing humorous in his voice.

"If it's dangerous, why are we going?"

"It's not dangerous if you stay with me." He pulled me back against him. "Promise me you'll stay with me."

"I promise. Do you think I want to get myself hurt?" I figured I could do my investigating with Levi at my side.

"Good. Ready to go?"

"Sure." I picked up my purse from the couch. "Are we driving or flying?"

"What would you prefer?" he whispered in my ear.

I turned in his arms. "Take a guess."

"Flying it is." He took off his jacket and started unbuttoning his shirt.

"If it's easier we can drive…"

"Yes, because taking off my shirt is so much work." We walked outside, and I waited for Levi to wrap his arms around me. I loved flying with him. As weird as it sounds, I rarely felt safer. I knew he'd never drop me.

Fighting the wind, I kept my eyes wide open. Levi flew low enough that I could watch the streets whiz by below. I watched as people walked around on the way to their New Year's plans completely unaware of what was happening above them. The air was crisp but not freezing despite our altitude.

It was after nine when we arrived at the Eiffel Society. Levi and the rest of the group landed in the shadows of the building, and Hailey and I waited as the guys put back on their shirts and jackets. Hailey's dress had left plenty of room for her wings. Levi took my hand and led me toward the entrance. Even though I'd passed the club tons of times, it was still amazing to walk up the elaborate staircase that wound its way up from the street to the front door.

"Sir." A bouncer bowed his head when we reached the door.

"How's the crowd?" Levi asked.

"Large but manageable. We've had some humans trying to crash, but we've been strict with the list."

"Good. I don't want a problem." Levi led me forward. Out of the corner of my eye, I watched the bouncer check something off his list. I wondered what I was listed as. I was almost positive it wasn't Allie Davis. It was probably prince's mate. Or maybe princess. Levi helped me out of my coat so we could check it. No one else needed one, even Hailey left hers back at the apartment. She'd only worn it so her dad wouldn't see her short dress.

We moved toward the main room. It took me a minute to take everything in. Loud music pulsated from every corner, while bare light bulbs and chandeliers hung down from the ceiling. The room was large, with a dance floor, stage, and plenty of tables. It was a mix between a restaurant and a bar. Levi tightened his hold on my waist as he led me over to a table in the corner. I had a feeling it was the VIP section. He pulled out a chair and pushed me in. Hailey sat down on my other side. Jared and Owen took the remaining seats. We didn't even have to order drinks. A waiter materialized out of nowhere and brought us a bottle of Dom Perignon.

"We're not waiting until midnight for the champagne?" I watched as the waiter filled my glass.

"Why wait?" Levi leaned over to kiss me on the cheek. His lips remained a moment longer than necessary and the extra seconds of contact made me shiver.

As soon as the waiter left, Levi made a toast. "To a new year, a new night, and this amazing girl on my right. To Allie."

I bit back a smile. If anyone else thought it was funny that he was toasting to me, they didn't show it. Everyone sipped their champagne.

"So everyone here is a shifter?" I watched a sea of dancers move by. It was an interesting crowd. Although almost everyone was dressed formally, a decent number of party goers were in masquerade attire. I wondered if that was usual.

"Almost entirely. We let in a few witches this year, and one other Pteron mate, but that's it."

"Isn't that boring for Pterons though?" Pterons were only supposed to date humans. The only one who seemed to mind this rule was Hailey. She had a thing for at least one shifter.

"I don't know, is this boring?" Levi looked at his friends.

"No, I don't mind taking a night off." Jared winked.

I rolled my eyes. "Ugh. You really are gross. Do you think you'll ever date the same girl for more than a day?"

He shrugged. "If I meet the right girl, sure."

Owen laughed. "Yeah right. Good luck with that."

"You should talk—" Jared stopped himself. Probably deciding it wasn't worth setting Owen off. Poor Owen was still brokenhearted over a girl who ran from him when she found out what he was.

I sipped my champagne guiltily. It was hard to enjoy a night out when Jess was being held hostage. Levi could tell me about the importance of waiting till the right moment a hundred more times—I still wanted to get her out immediately. It was impossible to be calm.

"What's wrong?" Levi put a hand on my leg. I hated how perceptive he was getting about me.

"I'm just worried about Jess." I enjoyed the way his strong hand felt on my leg. It gave me a comfort I was learning to appreciate more and more.

"How is worrying going to help? Try to relax, I promise it's going to be okay."

"It should be me, not her."

"No, it shouldn't!" He slammed his free fist on the table, spilling several glasses of champagne in the process.

"Wow, man. Chill out," Jared said carefully. Even he understood the danger of pushing Levi too much when he was angry.

"Then tell her to not say stuff like that. It shouldn't be you." I didn't need to look at Levi to know his eyes were probably darkening.

I touched his arm. "I just mean she shouldn't be punished. None of this is her fault."

"It's not yours either." He grabbed a napkin and cleaned up some of the champagne that had spilled on the table in front of me.

"Do you want to dance?" It seemed like the best way to calm him down. Funny how it went from him comforting me to the other way around.

"Yes." He got up and took my hand. He led me onto the dance floor. "I'm sorry."

"It's okay. I know this is stressing you out too." I wrapped my arms around his neck as he put his around me.

He leaned down and gently kissed me on the lips. "I love you, Al. I can't even think about losing you."

"People love Jess too."

"I know. Her boyfriend is with her. If the Blackwells were going to hurt her, they wouldn't have him there."

I rested my head against his chest. The music was fast, but we were barely moving. "I hope you're right." I kept telling myself that Toby would never hurt Jess or her boyfriend. Emmett had been one of Toby's best friends in high school.

"I am." Moving his hands to my hips, Levi made us move faster. Before long, I got lost in the rhythm of the music and having Levi's body pressed against mine.

We danced until I needed a break. "Let's have some more champagne." He let me lead him back to the table. He was grinning like a little kid. I loved how happy I could make him sometimes.

"It's about time." Jared poured champagne into both of our glasses without us asking.

"Oh, you missed us?" I took a sip.

"Of course, Princess. Although you two looked like you were having fun." He nodded toward the dance floor.

"We were." Levi put his hand back in its usual spot on my leg.

"Aren't you guys going to dance?" I asked.

"With who?" Jared finished off his glass.

"Each other. Or, come on, there are plenty of girls here. You really won't dance with other shifters?"

"Not if I have a choice," Jared grumbled.

I nabbed a strawberry from the fruit salad that had somehow materialized on our table while we danced. I assumed Hailey was behind it—I couldn't imagine Jared or Owen ordering fruit. "I'd ask you to dance, but Levi's going to veto that."

Levi shifted slightly closer to me. "Yes, I will."

"What about me? Do I get to dance with Allie?" Hailey set down her empty glass.

"Will you stay somewhere in this area?" Levi grabbed another strawberry for me before I even finished the first.

"Yes, we'll stay in sight. Normally I'd give you a hard time, but we do need to be careful with Allie." Hailey turned to me. "No offense."

"I get it." I ate the second strawberry before getting out of my chair again.

Hailey and I walked onto the dance floor hand in hand and danced for a while. Levi watched us with an amused expression on his face. I knew he liked how close Hailey and I were. I think it made him feel more secure that my best friend was a Pteron. It gave me another reason to feel like part of The Society. Well, one of my best friends. My other best friend was a kidnapping victim.

My stomach turned. Dancing didn't seem like so much fun.

"I need to use the bathroom." The champagne had gone right through me.

"Sure. Let's tell Levi first."

We walked back over to the table in a way that felt like checking in. Even though I knew it was necessary, there was still something belittling about it.

He kissed my cheek. "Come right back though."

"We will."

15

There was a huge line in the bathroom, but Hailey pulled us all the way to the front. I'm guessing people figured out who we were, because no one got mad. After washing my hands, I couldn't find Hailey. I assumed she'd finished first, so I walked out of the bathroom to look for her. I'd only made it a few steps when two strong arms came around my waist. They weren't Levi's.

"Hello, gorgeous." The voice was low and husky. It sounded off from how the owner of it usually sounded, but it had to be him.

"Toby?"

"Come with me quietly." His lips brushed against my ear.

"What are you doing here?" I struggled in his arms, but he wouldn't let go.

"I said quietly." His arms tightened.

Every part of me wanted to scream for help, but it might have been my one chance to get Jess back. "Okay."

We moved into a shadowed hallway behind the bathrooms, and I finally looked up at his face. Even without the dim lighting, I wouldn't have seen much. He was wearing a masquerade mask. "Let Jess go."

"I will, eventually." He put a hand on my hip. I fought the urge to shrug him off. I needed any information I could get. "I swear you get more beautiful every time I see you. And this dress." He moved his hand around to my back. "This dress is killing me."

I tensed as his hand continued to move down. "What the hell is going on? Why do you have her?"

He laughed. It wasn't the laugh I remembered. It was colder somehow. "I thought we already discussed this, sweetheart."

16

"You want me to come willingly. What does that even mean?"

"So he hasn't told you anything, has he?"

"Anything about what? At least he told me he wasn't human. That's more than you can say." I struggled to keep my voice down.

He ran a hand down my cheek. "Oh, Allie. My sweet, Allie. I was waiting until the right moment." This wasn't Toby—not the Toby I remembered at least. It felt like someone had taken over his body—except for the way he said my name. That was the same.

"And when would the right moment have been?"

"Our wedding night." His voice softened. Like the way he said my name, it gave me hope that the real Toby was still in there.

"Our wedding night? You were delusional enough to think we'd get married?"

"It wasn't a delusion. I knew it from the first time I kissed you. I've been waiting years to really have you."

"Really have me?"

"Has Levi not shown you what real sex with a Pteron is? I assumed he'd be doing it every chance he could. I would."

"You mean while transformed?"

"Of course. It was always good. So good. But it's going to be so much better."

He reached for my left hand, looking at my ruby ring with distaste. "I would have shown you who I really was once you were wearing my ring."

"Your ring? You have a ring too?"

"Yes. You'll be wearing it soon enough."

"What?"

"We don't have much time. I'm sure he's already looking for you. I just needed to see you and give you a message." He rested his hand on my hip.

"Message?"

"Have you been thinking about our kiss?" He pulled me against him. If I had any doubt about what was on his mind, it was made crystal clear by what was currently pressed against me.

I shook my head.

"I've been thinking about it constantly. I already knew you still had feelings for me, but it was nice to get a physical reminder."

"I felt nothing. You kissed me against my will."

"That's not true. You wanted the kiss, Allie. If you'd be honest with yourself, you want more. You want me—all of me. Do you remember what it used to feel like? Do you remember what it was like to have me on top of you, to have me in—"

I slapped him across the face. I used his momentary surprise to step away from him. He touched his cheek and grinned. "I love this feisty side. Things are going to be so much more fun the second time around."

"Was that your message?"

"No. My message is that I'm still setting things up. When I tell you it's time, you come home to me willingly. I'll let Jess go, and your life can go back to normal."

"Normal? But you said I'd have your ring. Isn't it the same thing? I'd be trading one prison for another?" I said the words even though I didn't quite view my relationship with Levi that way anymore.

"It won't be a prison, it will be a palace." He inched toward me again. His closeness felt stifling.

"You can't break the bond I have with Levi. This ring isn't coming off." I touched my ruby ring. It had become such a constant part of me. I wondered if it was like wearing a wedding ring, or if it was something more because you could never take it off.

"I'd tell you I hope you figure out what you are on your own, but I'm kind of looking forward to telling you myself—when I finally take you to bed again." He put his hand back on my hip. "God, I want you right now."

"Please just let Jess go."

"Not a chance, Allie. Go have fun with your friends. You won't be seeing too much more of them—I can promise you that. Oh, and tell anyone I was here, and we will hurt her."

"What?"

"Right now we're treating her well, but that can change at any time."

"Why can't I tell?"

"This visit needs to stay our little secret." Without warning, he disappeared into the crowd, and I was left even more worried and confused about what to do than before.

I walked back toward the bathrooms. Hailey was waiting outside with the guys next to her. She ran over and hugged me. There was panic all over her face. "Where the hell were you?"

"I'm sorry, I went looking for you."

Levi moved in front of Hailey. "Next time, wait."

"I will." I looked down, not wanting to meet his eyes. I didn't want to lie to him, but I was afraid Toby would somehow find out if I didn't.

"It's almost midnight. Let's get some more champagne." He led me back toward our table. I didn't complain. I couldn't stop thinking about Toby's words and his confidence that I'd get back with him. What was he talking about when he asked whether I knew what I was? I needed more information, and the one person I knew wouldn't give it to me was currently holding my hand.

Chapter Three

Despite the insanity of the night, I did get my New Year's kiss. Levi made sure to make it memorable. He stopped to grab my coat, a detail I would have forgotten, before leading me outside a few minutes before midnight.

"This is going to be our best year yet." He leaned in, planting a tiny kiss on my lips. "The best."

The fireworks started as he kissed me again. By the time I stepped back, breathless, the show was in full force. "I didn't know New Orleans did fireworks on New Year's." I had to talk loudly over the explosive noise.

He grinned. "They don't."

"You mean—this is you?" I pointed at the incredible show above us. The colors were fantastic, and I felt like a kid again waiting for each set.

"I wanted it to be memorable." He took my hand.

I glanced around, surprised I didn't hear any cheering or anything. "Wait, why isn't anyone else out here?"

"They were instructed to keep everyone else inside until 12:05."

As if on cue, people started flooding out.

I laughed. "Right on time."

"Exactly. Want to go home?" I wasn't surprised when he asked me. The kiss let me know there was much more to come. I needed him. The only thing that was going to calm me down was a night with Levi. It might even save me from the killer headache I could feel forming. I'd been getting them every few days since leaving for Vermont, and Levi had a knack for getting rid of them just by being near me.

"Yes. Definitely, yes. We just need to call Hailey."

"I already told everyone we were leaving."

"How'd you know I'd want to?"

He started to button my coat. I hadn't bothered with it when we came out. "Great minds think alike."

***

"I've been waiting for this all night." Levi unzipped my dress, letting it fall onto the floor of his room.

"You aren't the only one." I unbuttoned his shirt and pulled his white t-shirt over his head. I ran my hands down his chest, still marveling at how muscular he was.

"Happy New Year to me." He unclasped my bra and pulled down my panties at the same time. His eyes devoured my naked body, and I unbuttoned his pants, tugging off his boxers. He stepped out of his pants and shorts before taking a seat on his bed. He pulled me onto his lap, and I wrapped my arms around his neck.

I was glad no one else was home. It was impossible to be quiet with Levi. It was made even harder when I felt his firm wings under my hands. Usually he warned me when he was going to transform, but he surprised me. I opened my eyes to see his eyes completely black. He moved faster, and I dug my nails into his back.

He brought me over the edge and joined me moments later. I leaned forward into his chest. He kissed the top of my head. "How did I make it my whole life without you?"

"Hard to believe, huh?"

"You know it."

We got under his sheets, and I hoped the feeling of physical completeness would be enough to get me to sleep. At least my headache was gone.

***

Two hours later, I was still wide awake and incredibly thirsty. I needed a glass of water. I slipped out of Levi's arms and legs. It was no easy feat. He had me all tangled up. If I opened my suitcase I'd wake Levi, so I grabbed my underwear and Levi's dress shirt. I'd heard everyone come in, but the only one staying in the living room was Hailey, and she was probably sound asleep.

I eased the door open quietly and closed it as silently as I could. Hailey left a lamp on, but the apartment was eerily quiet. I poured myself a glass of water from the pitcher in the fridge.

"Allie?" Hailey called sleepily.

"Yeah. Sorry if I woke you up."

"It's not a problem." She sat up. "But, uh, nice outfit."

I laughed and took a seat on the couch next to her, using her blanket to cover my legs. "I didn't want to wake Levi opening my suitcase."

"You know you could probably unpack. I'm sure Levi would be thrilled to give you some drawer space."

"I'm not moving in with him. I like living with you."

"You don't have to totally move in…"

"Do you want your own room or something?"

"No. Of course not!" She looked offended.

"I was just checking."

"Are you doing okay? Are you really just out here for water?"

"Would you be mad if I told you I wanted you to wake up?"

She laughed. "No. What's going on?"

I took a moment to gather my thoughts. Suddenly the red and blue checkered fleece blanket seemed really interesting. Eventually I looked up. "Were you really joking about the Pteron magnet thing?"

"Yes, I was kidding."

"But is it possible…" I had to know.

"Isn't anything possible?"

"Hailey. Come on." I sipped my water.

"I don't know. Why don't you ask Levi?"

"I can't. Every time I ask him anything about it, it somehow goes back to my sex life with Toby." I shuddered. I still couldn't believe Toby had been there earlier that night.

"Call Helen. If anyone knows, she would."

"Helen? How can I even bring it up?" The thought of asking Levi's mom hadn't crossed my mind.

Hailey shrugged. "I don't know. It's the middle of the night and that's the best I can come up with."

I set down my empty glass on the coffee table. "Thanks. I'll talk to her." The more I thought about it, the better it sounded.

"Did you girls forget to invite me to the slumber party?" Jared came out of his room in just a pair of boxers.

Hailey covered her eyes. "Put some clothes on."

"No, thanks. Are you girls hungry? I want pancakes."

I curled my legs up under me. "Pancakes? It's three a.m."

"And pancakes don't taste good at three a.m.?" He grinned.

"I am kind of hungry…" I admitted.

"Then come help, Princess."

I got up, forgetting how little I was wearing.

"Nice shirt." He pulled out a griddle and turned it on. "Funny, I thought Levi was wearing it earlier."

"At least I'm wearing more than underwear."

"It's my kitchen. I can wear what I want."

I glanced at Hailey. She'd joined us in the kitchen. "And you wonder why I won't move in?"

"Didn't Levi ask you about the houses?"

"Houses?"

"No, I didn't have the chance yet." Levi walked out of his room, still looking half asleep. He was also in nothing but boxers, and he put an arm around me. "You look really good in that."

"Yeah? I figured you wouldn't mind me borrowing it."

"It looks much better on you than on me." He took a seat on one of the stools at the counter, and pulled me onto his lap.

Hailey groaned. "Okay there is entirely too much naked maleness in here. Can you guys please put on clothes?"

"I hope you say that about every half naked guy." Owen strutted out. He, at least, had a shirt on.

"Can you grab the milk?" Jared asked.

"Sure." I started to move.

Levi pulled me back against him. "Owen will get it."

Jared grinned. "I guess I lost my assistant."

Levi leaned his chin against the top of my head. "Yes, you did."

"So what were you supposed to tell me about houses?"

"Anytime you're ready, we can start house hunting."

I turned on his lap. "House hunting? We're not ready for that."

"Do you think we're going to live here after the wedding?" he asked casually.

"Wedding?" I steadied myself on his shoulder. "We're still supposed to be doing that?"

"How did I find myself the one girl who doesn't want to get married?"

"That's not true. I want to, but it's just so soon." I never planned on getting married young, especially not before graduating from college.

"We have months, don't worry about it."

With everything else going on, I decided to drop it. My stomach grumbled.

"Throw some blueberries in, would you?" Levi remembered how much I loved blueberry pancakes—he'd earned himself some extra points.

Chapter Four

"Am I in trouble?" Levi stood in the doorway of his room with his car keys dangling from his fingers.

"Why would you be in trouble?" I tapped my foot impatiently. I was already ten minutes late, thanks to my inability to resist Levi.

"What other reason would you have to spend the day with my mom? You're obviously upset and want to get her to take your side or something."

I laughed. I couldn't help it. "Is it impossible to believe I just want to get to know my future mother-in-law?" It was weird using that term, but I had accepted we were going to be married eventually.

Levi didn't miss the importance of me using the title either. "Mother-in-law, huh? Just for that, I'll give you the benefit of the doubt."

I moved to push past him but he caught me and spun me around to look at him. "Are you absolutely sure you don't want me to hang out with you both?"

"Levi?" I laced my fingers with his.

"Yes?"

"I'm spending the afternoon with your mother. You are not invited, and nothing you can say will change that."

"Funny thing to say to your ride."

"Do you want me to get someone else to drive me? I'd take my own car, but wait—I'm not allowed."

"I thought you agreed it's for the best right now?"

I let go of his hands. "I do agree, but don't get all annoying about driving me places."

He smiled. "You ready, my lady?"

"Yes. I'm ready."

***

"Allie, honey. I'm so glad you called." Helen opened the door to welcome us in. I'd been over to the Laurent house more times in the last week than I'd ever been before. I'm pretty sure Robert thought interrogating his future daughter-in-law at his house was more acceptable than dragging me down to his office at the hotel. He kept asking me questions about Toby. I don't think any of my answers were what he was looking for.

"I'm sorry we're late." I wasn't necessarily an early bird, but I hated keeping people waiting—well, except for Levi. It was fun to annoy him sometimes by taking a while to get ready.

Levi moved past me into the entryway. "It's my fault. She's a hard girl to say goodbye to."

Helen raised an eyebrow. "I'll pretend you aren't eluding to what I know you are. Have a nice afternoon, Levi."

A look of shock crossed Levi's face. "Are you kicking me out?"

"Of course not. You're welcome to go up to your room or to visit your father's study. We'll be in my sitting room." Helen took my arm and led me away. I glanced over my shoulder and blew Levi a kiss.

He pretended to catch it. "Call me when you're done excluding me. Preferably before dinner."

Helen's sitting room was done in different shades of beige and pink. It screamed woman's space, and I liked it. It was in sharp contrast to the colder, more formal rooms of the main living space. After gesturing for me to take a seat on a comfortable looking love seat, she closed the door and poured two glasses from a pitcher. "I made mimosas."

I accepted my glass. "Oh, great. Thanks." It wasn't even three o'clock, but I knew a drink would make the conversation easier.

"How are you holding up? I know your friend's situation is upsetting, and finding out about your high school boyfriend must have been quite a shock." She smiled sympathetically.

"I'm doing all right. I just feel guilty. Here I am living my life like nothing's wrong while Jess is being held against her will."

"Living your life like nothing's wrong? You don't honestly believe that, do you?" She smoothed out a non-existent wrinkle in her blue dress.

"Maybe I'm just used to it."

"That's not entirely a bad thing, you know."

"I know."

Helen sipped her drink. "So what brought you here today? Not that you ever need a reason to visit with me."

I let out a deep breath. "I'm hoping you can help me with something."

She placed her glass on the side table next to her. "I'm listening."

I decided to just lay it out there. "Is it really a coincidence that the only two guys I've been with are both Pterons?"

"By been with, I assume you mean slept with."

I'm sure I blushed. It was weird talking about sex with Levi's mom. "Yes."

"It probably is. It might also be that you're attracted to men with Pteron attributes. They tend to be strong, virile, adventurous."

"Toby isn't adventurous. He's the opposite."

She crossed her legs and leaned forward slightly. "Are you sure that wasn't just because he thought you wanted it that way?"

I pondered the idea. "Maybe...I don't know."

"And under the same theory, Pteron men would be attracted to the same kind of woman. Strong, confident, sexy, attractive."

"A lot of girls fit that description."

She nodded. "Something tells me that wasn't the answer you were looking for."

"Is there another answer?"

"Maybe. I wish I could tell you more, but I honestly don't know. There may be one person that does." She leaned back.

"Who?"

"Robert's mother." By the look on Helen's face, she didn't have a great relationship with Levi's grandmother.

"Do you think she'd talk to me?"

"Not without some persuasion."

"Persuasion?" I took another sip of my mimosa.

"I can take care of that part." Helen tried to hide a smile.

"Where does she live? When can we see her?"

"She lives out on a plantation about a hundred miles from here. I'll see if I can set something up for next week."

"Should I be nervous?"

"Yes."

"Thanks for the honesty."

"She's not the easiest woman to get along with." Helen picked up her glass but didn't drink from it.

"I really appreciate your willingness to do this for me, then."

"Considering everything you've done for this family, I'd say you deserve it. Besides, I want to know as much as you do."

I doubted she wanted to know quite as much, but I appreciated the sentiment.

"Thank you." I set my empty glass aside.

"Not to change the topic suddenly, but I was going to invite you over soon anyway. Has anyone talked to you about the ball?"

"Hailey mentioned it once."

"Did she explain its significance?"

"No. She really just mentioned it briefly."

"The annual ball is thrown by our family every winter. The guest list is tight, only the most elite members of the community, supernatural or otherwise, are invited. It's a chance to celebrate the year and bring the different groups together. This year will be extra special though." Helen became animated as she talked.

"Why?"

"It will be the first time the crown prince will be bringing his mate."

"How is this different from the party last summer?"

"That was an engagement party so to speak. This is more formal, more public." She sat forward again, like she was eager to get up. "I don't mean to worry you, but you'll be on display. Invitations are always in high demand, but we've reached record highs."

My stomach turned nervously. "They just want to meet me?"

"Yes. You're their future queen." She said queen with admiration. She unquestionably respected her position.

"Crazy."

"There are fun parts about the ball."

Anything fun sounded good. "Like?"

"Your dress. Would you like to see it? I'm not quite done, but I'm getting close."

"You're not quite done? Does that mean you're making it yourself?"

"In another life I would have been a designer. At least I get to make dresses for both of us now." She stood up. "I have it waiting in my sewing room next door."

Helen pushed open another door. It opened into a similarly decorated room, except this room had a sewing station, dress mannequins, and fabric swatches all over. I'd barely walked into the room when my eyes immediately went to a floor-length red gown. I moved toward it. "Is this my dress?"

"Yes. What do you think?" Helen asked apprehensively.

"It's gorgeous." It was. Made of satin, with a long train and a ruby embellished bodice, I'd never seen anything like it. "I can't believe you made this."

"Would you like to try it on? I'd like to do a fitting."

"I'd love to."

Helen carefully removed the dress from the mannequin. I looked around for a place to change, but realized quickly she expected me to do it in front of her.

I undressed self-consciously. "Should I leave my bra on?"

"The dress is backless, so I went ahead and sewed in cups. We'll see if you need to adjust them at all."

Helen helped me into the dress. The satin felt cold against my skin, but any complaints were lost when I caught a glimpse of myself in the mirror. "Wow."

"You may give Levi a heart attack."

"I may give myself one. This looks incredible." I ran my fingers over the delicate straps.

"I am so glad you like it." Helen beamed. "It's tradition that the queen and princess each have a lady in waiting as well as maids. The lady in waiting must be a Pteron. My lady in waiting is my sister-in-law. Is it safe to assume that you'd like Hailey to take the position?"

"Of course. Anyway I can have Hailey involved would be great, but what would she be doing exactly?"

"Her job is to help you in any way possible."

"It sounds like Hailey would just be doing what she always does."

"It's an honor as well as a duty."

"Then I'm sure she'll be thrilled."

"I assumed you'd select Hailey, so I've started on her dress. I didn't know her exact measurements, but I think I'm close." Helen pointed out a black gown. It had a red sash and a border of rubies around the neckline. "It's tradition that the lady in waiting also wear the family stone."

"It's beautiful."

"I think so too." She smiled. "Are you ready to change? I think I heard the boys come in."

"Levi and his father?"

"You can call him Robert. If it was up to him, you'd call him Dad."

"But why? It's not like he likes me."

Helen looked at me seriously. "Of course he does. He's thrilled with Levi's choice. Don't let his hard exterior fool you. The way he sees it, Levi settled down and he got a daughter. He always wanted a daughter. It just didn't work out that way."

"Oh." I didn't know what to say to that. I wasn't sure that I believed her. Robert didn't seem like the president of my fan club, and I certainly wasn't the president of his.

Helen helped me out of my dress, and I got back into my black skirt and sweater while she put it up. "Let's do another fitting next week. Maybe you can bring Hailey with you and any maids that you'd like."

I wanted to ask her about the rules relating to the selection of maids when we were interrupted by a knock on the door. "If it isn't my two favorite women in the world." Levi pulled me into a hug.

"What happened to waiting for my call?"

"It's been a few hours. I can only wait so long. Besides, my dad told me to show up for dinner."

"Oh, we're all having dinner tonight?" I was extra glad I'd opted for a skirt instead of jeans. The Laurents dressed formally.

Levi tightened his arms around me and whispered in my ear. "I already got him to promise to be on good behavior. This will not be like the last time."

"I hope not." The last Laurent family dinner I attended ended with Levi and I in a heated fight after his father suggested my education take a backseat to travel with Levi. It wasn't what Robert said as much as how he said it. He acted like my opinion didn't matter at all.

I followed Levi out into the hall.

"Looking lovely as usual, Allison." Robert still insisted on calling me Allison. I usually let it go, but I was feeling daring.

"I'd prefer if you'd call me Allie, *Dad.*"

Levi burst out laughing. I guess I should have warned him.

Robert smiled. "Since you've dropped my full name, I suppose I can drop yours." From the twinkle in his eye, I had a feeling that's all he was waiting for.

"Great."

"Is everyone ready for dinner?" Helen asked. I couldn't believe she could keep a straight face.

"Definitely." I followed her into the dining room, afraid that if I looked at Levi I'd start laughing.

Levi pulled out my chair before sitting down next to me. Robert poured us all a glass of wine.

"What do you think?" Robert watched as I took a sip of my wine.

"It's nice. Velvety."

"Do you know wine, Allie?"

What was this, a test? "Not incredibly well."

"We'll have to work on that, but this is actually one of our own."

"Your estate in France still produces wine?" I knew they had a vineyard, but I guess I assumed it was no longer running.

"Yes, it's still producing wine." He smiled. "Maybe Levi can take you for a visit sometime soon. I took Helen right before our coronation. She enjoyed it."

"How did you two meet?" This was the first time I'd heard Robert mention his early years with Helen.

Helen smiled at Robert over the table. "I was a freshman in college. Robert was in graduate school, and he swept me off my feet."

"So it was a whirlwind romance?" I sipped my wine.

Robert laughed. "Not as whirlwind as I wanted it to be. It took a few months to convince her I was the one." There was something so soft and vulnerable in the way he said it.

I unfolded my napkin and placed it on my lap. "It was worth the chase though, wasn't it? It probably made it better."

Levi squeezed my hand under the table. "A chase isn't all it's cracked up to be."

The remainder of the dinner was uneventful. Helen made a delicious chicken and rice dish. I guess she'd done most of the work before I arrived. I liked it enough that I planned to get the recipe. I thought we were home free when Robert smiled at us. "Before you kids go, I have a surprise for you."

I glanced at Levi. His face was blank.

"I'm sure you two are growing tired of sharing walls with Jared and Owen. I thought it was about time I gave you your engagement present."

"Engagement present?" Levi asked.

Robert pulled a set of keys out of his pocket. "It's the one on Audubon you were looking at with your mother. You know houses like that don't stay on the market long."

My sip of wine went done the wrong tube. I coughed.

"You okay?" Levi put a hand on my back.

I held up a finger to tell Levi to wait. After another moment, I was ready to talk. "You bought us a house?"

"Yes. It's currently in Levi's name. When you publicly take his name this summer, you can add yours as well." If I had any doubts before, I now knew for sure it was a bribe to get me to go along with the wedding.

Levi glanced at me one more time before returning his attention to Robert. "That was generous, Dad."

"It's nothing. You two deserve a proper home. After all, you'll be starting a family before you know it."

It's lucky I hadn't taken another sip. "Not anytime in the near future."

"Not until after the wedding, of course." Robert refilled his wine glass.

"Of course." What I wanted to say was, not until I'm at least twenty-one. Considering my nineteenth birthday was well over a month away, we had plenty of time.

Levi squeezed my hand under the table. "Would you guys mind if we left? I'm sure Allie is as excited as I am to check out our new home."

Helen removed the napkin from her lap, placing it on the table. "Of course. We took the liberty of furnishing it, but you can change anything you don't like."

"We?"

From the guilty expression on Helen's face, she was definitely in on the surprise. As long as there wasn't a nursery, complete with a crib, I would stay reasonably calm.

Chapter Five

"He bought us a house? Isn't that a bit excessive?" I didn't even wait for Levi to start the car before jumping in with the questions.

"Excessive for my dad is different than for other people."

I could relate. My dad was the one who bought me a Land Rover for high school graduation, but still a car was different from a multi-million dollar house.

"Do you want to at least look at it?" Levi pulled out onto the street.

I chose my words carefully. He actually looked hopeful. "We can look, but I'm still moving back into the dorm when it opens."

"Sounds good to me." He slowed down as he turned onto a beautiful tree-lined street. There was a wide median down the middle with large oak trees covered in dangling moss. We were only a few blocks from campus, and I'd gone for a walk in the neighborhood before, but I definitely never imagined I'd have a house there.

"Oh. My. God." My jaw dropped as Levi drove into the driveway of the large white house. It looked a lot like the Laurents' house, eerily like it, but at least it was several blocks away. Two huge southern oaks, and a large magnolia dominated the well-manicured lawn.

I didn't wait for Levi to open my door. I was out before he'd gotten around. "Wow, this place is huge."

"It's over 6,000 square feet." Levi watched for my reaction.

"A little over the top, don't you think?" I may have said it, but I was currently admiring the incredible exterior. Tall columns, extending both levels, gave the house a southern feel.

"Wait until you see the inside." He took my hand and walked up onto the front porch. I touched one of the large white columns while I waited for him to unlock the door.

The inside was nothing short of spectacular. Tall ceilings welcomed you into the foyer. I stopped to take off my boots, not wanting to mess up the gorgeous wood floors or the rugs waiting for us in the living room.

"I think all of the bedrooms are upstairs." Leave it to Levi to already be worried about the bedrooms.

"We haven't even seen the kitchen yet."

"Details, details." He smiled; probably glad to see me enjoying our house. Our house... crazy.

The kitchen was beautiful—all dark wood and light granite countertops. "I might actually cook if I had this kitchen."

He laughed. "Good to know—since you do have this kitchen."

I kept exploring—discovering several closed off sitting rooms and a study. The part that got me was the dining room. It had a table that could seat sixteen, but that wasn't the coolest part.

"Wow, is that a pool?" The huge windows taking up the entire back wall of the room provided a view of the backyard.

"Yes. And there's also a hot tub." He arched an eyebrow. "I'd love to check that out."

"Don't you want to go upstairs first?"

"Definitely." He took my hand again before heading up the grand staircase.

We peeked into a bedroom. "Is this ours?"

He grinned. "First of all, I'm so proud that you actually called a room ours, but no. If I remember correctly from the virtual tour, that's a guest suite." He continued down to the end of the hall and pushed open the door. "This is the master."

"Wow." The room was enormous with a four poster king-sized bed in the middle. The quilt and sheets were both in various shades of red. "I have to see the bathroom."

I ran my hand over the marble lining the edge of the soaking tub. "Okay, I change my mind."

"About?"

"I want to stay in the dorms during the week, but we can stay here on weekends."

He laughed before pulling me into his arms. "Does tonight count as a weekend since we don't have class tomorrow?"

"We don't have any of our stuff with us."

"My mom helped set this up. Do you really doubt she took care of the details?"

"Wait, like in the safe room?"

"Take a look."

I opened the door to the gorgeous shower that had more than enough room for two. Stepping in, I found my usual shampoo and body wash. "She's unbelievable."

"This was just their way of welcoming you to the family."

"Are you sure you weren't in on this?"

"No. I wish I had been. I can't take any credit." He put his hands on my hips.

"How did they do this so quickly?"

"You know my dad, it shouldn't surprise you." He ran his hands down my arm. "So what do you say?"

"About?"

"Want to stay here tonight?"

"I think I could be persuaded."

"Oh, I'll persuade you."

He picked me up and set me down on the counter. My skirt rode up slightly, and the cool marble countertop made me shiver. "You won't be shivering at the end of this."

"Is that a promise?" I slipped my hands under the front of his long sleeved shirt. His skin was warm as always.

"Yes." He moved his hands under my legs, warming me up.

"Don't you need your hands to persuade me?"

"Are you doubting I can do it without them?"

"Yes." Challenging Levi was only a good idea when it came to kissing and sex. He thrived under that kind of pressure.

"Challenge accepted." He leaned forward and kissed me. I pulled him closer, moving his hands further up my skirt in the process. He broke the kiss. "That's not using my hands. That's all you."

"Fine. Just get back to kissing me."

He did as I asked, but his lips didn't stay on my lips long before they moved to my earlobe and then my neck.

I pulled his shirt over his head and started unzipping his pants.

"Am I allowed to use my hands yet?"

"Not quite yet." I pushed down his khakis and slipped my hand just underneath the band of his boxers. "Aren't you glad I didn't promise to keep my hands to myself?"

He grinned. "Very."

I moved my hand so I could pull my sweater over my head before returning it to Levi and pushing his boxers out of the way. He stepped out of his pants and boxers, kicking them away. Using his mouth, he pulled one of my bra straps down and kissed my shoulder before moving to the other and doing the same thing.

"Would you like some help with that?" I whispered into his ear.

"Yes," he grunted.

I used my free hand to reach around and unclasp my bra. He didn't waste a second before his mouth claimed one of my breasts.

I moaned. "You passed the challenge. You can use your hands now."

Before I could process it, he had me off the counter and on our bed. "I'm more than happy to accept any challenge you throw at me, babe." He yanked down my skirt and pulled off my panties. "On top or under the covers?"

"Under. I want to see how soft the sheets are."

"I don't think you'll be worrying about the sheets." As he said it, he pulled back the quilt and top sheet, laying me down.

I reached my arms up and around his neck. "You are entirely too far away."

"Am I?" he said softly, teasingly.

"Yes."

"I'll have to change that." He positioned himself over me, transforming instantly.

"Are you going to transform every time?"

He didn't answer, and seconds later I didn't care.

***

"Are the sheets up to specification?" Levi ran a hand down my stomach.

"They're fantastic." I snuggled into them contentedly. Being with Levi was always amazing. "But you never answered my question."

"What question?"

"Are you going to transform every time now? I'm not complaining, but you don't even warn me anymore—and it's pretty intense."

"Oh. I didn't even realize I was doing it until after. I think it just happens naturally now."

"Is that what's supposed to happen?"

"I actually don't know...I wouldn't think so, but the only one I can really ask is my dad."

"No. Don't ask."

Levi laughed. "Do you mind it?"

"No. It just takes me a lot longer to recover. It's so powerful. My body feels like it's transforming somehow."

"Is that your way of telling me I need to give you a break?"

"Maybe just a little."

He kissed my forehead. "I'll stick to cuddling the rest of the night."

He lay on his back, and I rested my head on his chest. "I think I could get used to this house."

"Me too, as long as I get to go to sleep every night with you right where you are."

Chapter Six

"Where are you?" Hailey asked when I finally answered my phone.

"Good morning to you too." I propped up my pillow, still trying to wake up.

"I'm at the guys' place, and Owen says you and Levi never came home last night. Did you go down to the hotel or something?"

Levi chuckled. "Glad to know you're worried about us, Hailey."

It was still weird how well he could hear. He was lying on his back with his hands behind his head. Waking up with Levi was becoming one of my favorite parts of the day.

I smiled, loving the answer I was about to give. "We're actually at our house."

"Your house?"

"Yeah. The Laurents bought us a house. It's over on Audubon. It's pretty spectacular."

"I'd bet. I picked up bagels and coffee. Should I come over there?"

"Definitely." Bagels and coffee? Hailey knew me well. "You can bring Jared and Owen too."

"Gee, I'd love that." Hailey may have complained about her brother and Jared, but I think she enjoyed their company more than she let on. I did too.

"It's the large white house with the columns. See you in a few."

I sat up, pulling the blanket around me. "We need to get dressed."

Levi rolled over toward me. "You mean you don't want to welcome our first guests while you're naked?"

"Not exactly." I pulled on my clothes from the day before. Unlike the safe room, Helen hadn't stocked the room with clothes. I didn't mind, the toiletries were plenty.

***

"Okay, so where's my room?" Hailey's reaction to the house was similar to mine. She couldn't stop looking around at everything.

"You know, we didn't even finish checking out all the rooms last night." I finished the last bite of my cinnamon raisin bagel.

"I wonder what got you distracted?" Hailey nudged me with her shoulder.

I bit back a smile. "We looked into one other room."

"Shall we explore?" Hailey stood up.

"Sounds good." I turned to Levi. "See you later."

He waved before returning to a conversation with his friends.

We headed up the stairs. I ran my hand over the wood railing; every detail about the house was beautiful. If Robert wanted to find a way to bribe me—he'd succeeded.

"When are you moving out?" Hailey said it calmly, but I could tell she was worried.

"I'm not."

"Really?" Relief was clear on her face. "You're picking the dorm over this?"

"I told Levi we can stay here on the weekends."

She smiled. "Wow, that's so awesome."

"Did you think I was going to ditch my lady in waiting?"

"What?" Her expression was a mix of shock and excitement. "You can't be serious."

"Helen's already working on your dress. It's gorgeous."

She hugged me. "Oh my god. That's incredible. My parents—wow—oh my god."

When she pulled away, I thought I saw a tear run down her face. Hailey, crying?

"Who'd you think it would be? Did you think I was hanging out with other Pterons behind your back?"

"I figured they'd want you to pick someone more appropriate, like Michelle."

"More appropriate? That's ridiculous. Besides, the job of the lady in waiting is to do everything to help the princess. You already do that."

"What do the dresses look like?"

"You'll find out when you go for your first fitting."

She squealed. Wow, this was such a different side to Hailey.

"Dare I ask?" Levi asked from the top of the stairs.

"I was telling Hailey about her dress."

"I take it you're happy about the job?"

"Is that even a question?" Hailey was still giddy.

"I think I know who I want as my maids."

"Oh yeah?" Levi pushed open one of the doors. It was a library with the most comfortable looking reading nook I'd ever seen. Piled with pillows and cushions, the window bench vied with the upholstered chair and ottoman as the best seat in the house. If my life ever calmed down, I could picture myself spending hours in that room.

I sat down on the window seat. "I figure I should ask Michelle." Not only was her mother friends with Helen, but she'd been a huge help with my Art History exam. As long as she stopped treating Hailey rudely, I wouldn't mind spending time with her.

Levi nodded. "That would be smart."

"Can I ask Anne and Tiffany?" I said it fast because I wasn't sure what response I was going to get.

"They're just normal humans…"

"So? They're my friends."

"They do know about The Society." Hailey jumped in to help. "What's the problem?"

Levi shrugged. "Why not? Just get their measurements to my mom. You know she'll want their dresses to match."

"Thank you." I got up and kissed Levi on the cheek.

"Are you thankful enough to spend another night?"

"Maybe one more."

He put an arm around my waist. "Then you're very welcome."

***

Things were exactly the way we left them in our dorm room. My side was neat and orderly, and Hailey's still had clothes strewn on her chair and bed. I had to give it to Hailey, she kept the mess on her side.

"It's strangely nice to be back." Hailey moved a pair of jeans so she could sit on the end of her bed.

"I know what you mean. It doesn't take long for a new place to feel like home." I meant more than my dorm. It was hard to believe I'd never been to New Orleans before that previous summer.

"I haven't seen you without Levi yet." Hailey leaned back on her elbows. "What happened with Helen?"

"She didn't know much, but we're supposed to visit Levi's grandma next week."

"You're visiting Georgina?"

"Is that her name?"

"Yes. Wow, good luck."

"Is she that bad? Helen made her sound that way, but it's her mother-in-law so she's biased."

"Not as much bad as scary. But she's a few hours outside the city. Are you going to stay over?"

"Oh, I hadn't thought of that."

"Yeah, she's out in the middle of nowhere on her family's old plantation."

"How old is she?"

"Only seventy or so, and I think she's really with it. Just be prepared for her to tell you you're not good enough for Levi or something like that. She used to come into meetings and yell at girls for bad posture and stuff."

"At least I have that down." When your mom's a former model, she pushes the posture thing on you from a young age.

"You know what I mean."

"I know."

"Hello, neighbors!" Anne walked in. We never bothered to lock our door unless we were sleeping.

"Hey!" I got up and hugged her. I'd missed her carefree personality over the few weeks of break.

"How was Vermont, or should I not ask?"

Hailey hugged Anne next. "She's completely back with Levi, and they now have a multi-million dollar home together."

"What? How did I miss this?" Anne sat down on my bed.

"Do you want to tell her or should I?" Hailey asked.

I nodded toward the door. "Shouldn't we wait for Tiffany?"

As if she heard her name, Tiffany walked in. We all laughed.

"Would I be paranoid if I asked if you were laughing at me?" She looked exhausted, and I decided not to ask about her break. Tiffany was the kind of person that let you know what details she wanted to share.

"Not at you." I hugged her. "We were just talking about you, it was too perfect."

"Talking about good things, I hope."

Anne unzipped her sweatshirt. I couldn't blame her. The heat was on high in the dorm, and it seemed especially hot in my room. "They wouldn't spill about why she and Levi now own a mansion together."

"What?" Tiffany sat down on the floor in front of me. "I'm listening."

"You can tell it, Hail." Hailey had a gift for telling concise stories. I tended to say too little or go on forever.

Hailey cleared her throat like she was about to go into a long speech. "Allie's ex-boyfriend showed up in Vermont to try to woo her back."

"Woo? Where did you get that word?" I laughed.

"Do you want me to tell this story?"

"Sorry, go on."

"Somehow that made Allie realize just how special what she has with Levi really is. We came right back, and the two have been inseparable since."

"Aww, that's so sweet." Anne was such a romantic at heart, even if she pretended she wasn't.

"But, it's not that simple." I hated even having to think about the rest.

"Uh oh." Tiffany looked at me nervously. "What happened?"

"It turns out her ex is a Pteron and he kidnapped her best friend from high school in an attempt to get her back."

"Is that all of it?" Hailey looked at me.

"Pretty much." I took out my stress on a throw pillow. That poor thing had put up with a lot lately.

Anne's jaw dropped. "What? That's insane! Where's your friend?"

"Jared got some intel that she's fine. She's being kept in a house somewhere. Jared and Levi say they can't get her until they find out more. Otherwise, she'll just be at risk again." The part I didn't say was that Anne and Tiffany would be at risk too. Anyone who knew me probably was. There was no way I was letting any more of my friends get pulled into the mess that was my life.

"Have you thought about how random it is that you've dated two Pterons?" Tiffany said carefully.

"It can't be random. I need to find out why." I had a feeling it was the key to figuring out how to protect everyone around me.

Chapter Seven

"What do you know about Georgina?" I asked Jared as we waited for our professor in Organic Chemistry II. It was the first day, but I knew the professor would jump right in because it was just a continuation of the semester before.

"Levi's grandma? Not too much. She's a pretty intense lady. Actually, she kind of reminds me of you." He smiled at a blonde who was eyeing him from across the aisle before turning his attention back to me.

"What?"

"You both scare me."

I lightly punched his arm. "I do not scare you."

"She says after she assaults me."

"If I assaulted you, you'd know it."

"Is that a threat?" He smirked.

"Do you feel threatened?"

"Very." He leaned over and whispered. "You are a very threatening princess."

"Be careful or I'll beat you up with my tiara."

"Just don't break it. That thing has been in the Laurent family for years."

"What? I was joking. I actually have a tiara?" I pulled out the brand-spanking-new light weight laptop Levi bought me for Christmas.

"Of course. Helen hasn't showed you yet? You get to wear it at the ball."

"Interesting." A tiara made the princess stuff seem a whole lot more real.

"You're such a girl."

"As compared to what?"

"Nothing. I've just never seen your girly side. You're all teeth and nails usually." He held up his hands like claws.

"Wasn't I the one you called weak a few months ago?"

"Weak and girly are two different things. Aren't you going to turn it on?" He gestured to my laptop.

"I tried."

He laughed. "You can't figure out how to turn on your computer?"

"Don't laugh. Fix it."

"Didn't you try it out?" He pressed a button I could have sworn I'd already tried. Of course, the thing booted instantly.

"No. Levi said he loaded everything for me."

Jared shook his head. "At least you trust him again."

"Shouldn't I trust him?"

"Of course. I'm just saying, it took a while."

"As it should have. He didn't deserve easy forgiveness."

The blonde glared at me, clearly getting the wrong impression about us. I just smiled back at her.

"I bet you're still getting him to make it up to you."

"Dare I ask what you're implying?"

"You know exactly what I'm implying. I know about your challenges."

"What!" I said it louder than I meant to.

"What's the problem?" He grinned from ear to ear.

"Levi told you that?" I could barely breathe, I was so mortified.

"Yeah, so?"

"He's dead. He's absolutely one hundred percent dead." I gritted my teeth. If Levi had been within arm's reach, he'd have had a red mark on his face in the shape of my hand.

"Come on, Levi tells me everything. It's not a big deal."

"Not a big deal? I hate you both." I picked up my laptop and tote bag and moved over a few seats.

Of course, Jared followed and he was laughing. "Do you think I care? I'm just glad you're finally giving Levi some. He was such an ass when you were holding out on him."

I turned around. Some nerdy looking guy behind us was watching us with interest. I faced forward again. "Shut up. Not another word."

Thankfully, the professor came in. I'd never been more interested in aromatic hydrocarbons before.

Class went by at a snail's pace, but it gave me time to calm down. Or so I thought.

"Are you still mad?" Jared asked as he followed me out of the room.

"What do you think?"

"I didn't do anything."

"No, but your buddy did." I still couldn't believe Levi would humiliate me like that. What else was he telling his friends?

"My buddy? You're his mate."

"Don't remind me."

Jared laughed again. "Please don't make a huge deal out of this. Who cares that you like sex with him transformed and your favorite position is—"

I pushed him. "Don't say another word to me. Not one word."

I pulled out my phone and texted Levi. *You are in so much trouble.* I put my phone away. Thankfully, my second class was on the same quad. I reached the building and turned to glare at Jared. "You can leave. I'm sure Owen's waiting inside."

"No can do. I need visual confirmation."

I put a hand on my hip. "Visual confirmation?"

"Chill out, I'll call him." He pulled his phone from his pocket.

As expected, Owen walked outside. "Hey, couldn't find the room?"

"Ha ha. So funny. Your friend here said he needed visual confirmation of my next babysitter."

Jared shook his head. "Be careful, Owen, she's a live one today."

"It's your fault." I brushed past both of them and into the building.

I found a seat and set up my laptop. I had no trouble getting it out of sleep mode, thank goodness.

"What's up with you?" Owen tossed his backpack on the floor and took a seat in the desk next to mine. I was actually really excited for our Southern History class to start. You don't learn much about that subject when you grow up in New York.

"No comment."

My phone vibrated. I had no doubt who was texting me. *What did I do?*

Our private life is exactly that, private. If you're not man enough to keep it to yourself, then you're not man enough to have one. I smiled, satisfied that I'd said my piece—until I saw him.

Owen leaned over me to read my phone screen. The smile that spread across his face confirmed that Levi had been blabbing to him too.

"If you so much as mention my sex life, I'm going to slap you."

"Not saying a word."

"Good."

I got another text just as the professor walked in. *Good thing I'm a Pteron then ;) Love ya, babe.*

Was he serious? That was his response? I took a deep breath. There was nothing I could do until after class.

My professor was fantastic. She was young and obviously passionate about the subject. I was already excited to pick a term paper topic.

She let us out early, and Owen walked me back to my dorm. "Off the record, Levi should have kept his mouth shut."

"Thanks. I appreciate that."

"What do you appreciate?" Hailey joined us. She'd just gotten out of class too.

"I'll tell you all about it upstairs."

"This isn't good, is it?"

Owen smiled. "Not for Levi."

"What has the idiot done now?"

"Idiot?" Owen snapped. "Watch it, Hailey."

"Oh shut up, Owen." Hailey took my arm, and we headed inside. She waited until the door was closed to start asking questions.

"What did he do?"

I tossed my bag on my chair. "He just blabbed about our sex life in vivid detail to his two goons."

"Ugh, he's so dumb sometimes." She kicked off her flip flops. It was fifty degrees and she was wearing sandals. I'd just taken off boots. "What are we going to do?"

"I love how you say we."

"I'm always on your side. What kind of punishment is he getting?" She got a gleam in her eye. She felt bad for me, but she loved scheming.

"I'm not sure yet, but it's got to be good. Look at this text." I opened the message and tossed my phone to her.

"So are you thinking he gets a freeze out, public humiliation…"

"Oh, he's getting a freeze out, but I need to come up with something better." I sat down cross-legged on my bed.

Hailey laughed. "I love you, Allie."

"Yeah, I love you too."

Hailey still had my phone when I got another text. "Oh, you're going to love this."

She tossed my phone back. I caught it and looked at the screen. *Lunch at 12?*

You are so delusional.

Why?

I'm not answering that. If you can't figure it out, ask your idiot friend, Jared. You already tell him everything.

I won't do it again.

You're going to have to do better than that. No lunch.

I put my phone down.

Hailey leaned over my shoulder. "Since you're free for lunch, do you want to grab some? I'm starving."

"Absolutely. Are Tiffany and Anne around?"

"I don't know their new schedules yet."

I laughed. "So ridiculous. It's the first day of school and you don't have their classes memorized."

We grabbed our keys and IDs, and knocked next door. There was no answer, but I heard music. "Do you think Anne has someone in there?"

"Technically it could be Tiffany..." Hailey grinned. Tiffany was too good of a girl for that.

Hailey knocked again. "If you're not having sex, we're heading to the U.C. for lunch." Everyone called the University Center by the acronym.

The door flew open and a red-faced Tiffany gaped at us. There was a guy sitting on her bed.

"Oh, sorry. We thought you were Anne," Hailey stammered.

Tiffany turned an even deeper shade of red. "We weren't doing anything. This is Cam, we're just getting started on a project."

"A project, eh?" Hailey tried to keep a straight face. I nudged her.

"Oh, cool. Sorry to interrupt." I backed up.

"You didn't interrupt."

"Okay, well, we'll leave you alone anyhow." Hailey took my arm, and we headed to the stairs.

"Do you think they were fooling around?" I asked.

"Who knows? It's not a bad thing. It's better than her still having a crush on Jared."

"Good point."

We walked over to the U.C. without running into any Pterons. I don't think I could have handled any more of them.

Chapter Eight

"You can't be mad at me again." Levi was leaning against the wall of our dorm when Hailey and I came home from dinner that night. I hated to admit it, but he looked so sexy with his arms crossed and that scowl. I just wanted to kiss it off his face.

"I can't?"

"No. I hate fighting with you. I thought we were done with that."

"Then why'd you go blabbing about our personal life to your friends?"

"I'm going to let you guys talk this one out." Hailey hightailed it inside.

"I didn't think it mattered."

"You mean you didn't think I'd find out."

He reached out, grabbed my hand, and pulled me closer. I let him. "Is it really a bad thing that I like to brag about how amazing you are?"

"Uh huh, that's what it's about."

"It is. Jared gave me hell the whole time you were holding out on me. It's only natural I want to shove it back at him."

"I'm still mad at you, but—"

"Would it help if I promised I won't do it again?"

"I was trying to tell you that I'm sure you'll find a way to make it up to me."

He grinned. "What are you doing now?"

"Good try. Not tonight. Maybe this weekend."

"All right, date night at our place?"

"You like saying that, don't you?"

"Our place? Of course I do, but so do you."

"Says who?"

"Says the look on your face. You may be making me wait until the weekend, but if you weren't so determined to win every argument, you'd be getting into my car right now."

"Tell yourself whatever you want." I crossed my arms.

"Can I at least get a kiss good night?"

"Sure." I leaned up and kissed him on the cheek. Then I thought better of it and left a light kiss on his lips. "Goodnight, Levi."

He groaned. "You can't do this to me. I need you."

"If you can't handle two nights without me in your bed, you've got problems." Classes had started on a Wednesday again. I liked beginning with a short week.

"Did you have to add the 'in my bed' part?" He ran a hand down my arm. "You can't put that picture in my head and leave me hanging."

"I'm supposed to be mad at you."

He smiled hesitantly. "Allie Davis, are you actually giving in to me?"

"Maybe…but only if I can go back to being mad at you in the morning."

"You're asking whether you can go back to being mad at me after spending the night with me?"

"Yes." I tried to keep a straight face but a smile broke through. I was annoyed at him, but he was just too much for me. With everything else going on, I didn't have the strength to fight it. Besides, Levi was the only one who could make my headaches go away. I'd use any rationalizations I had to.

"Do you want to grab a change of clothes?"

"Yes."

"What are we waiting for?"

Hailey turned from her laptop when we walked in. Her eyes immediately went to our joined hands. "So much for our revenge."

"Don't worry, Hail. She's going back to being mad at me in the morning."

"I really don't get you two, but I don't think it matters. I'm guessing I'll see you in the a.m., Allie?"

"You don't mind, do you?"

"Nope. Anne's been trying to talk me into going to the Boot tonight with her. I may just have to give in."

"Want us to walk you?" I tossed a few sets of clothes into a small duffel. I figured I might as well have extras.

"No, I think I can handle the one minute walk alone." She rolled her eyes. Sometimes I forgot she wasn't human and didn't need to worry about safety the way the rest of us did.

"All right, have fun."

"You too. Don't forget to be mad at him again in the morning." She grinned.

***

Any thought of being mad at Levi disappeared when I woke up in his arms Thursday morning. I believed him. He really didn't think he was doing anything wrong— sometimes it was frustrating being with someone so used to getting and doing anything he wanted.

I'd tried to sleep in a little later while he showered, but a phone call cut my sleep short. "Helen?"

"Hi, Allie. I'm calling to see if you'd like to take a drive out to see Georgina on Friday afternoon."

"Oh, yeah that would be great." This was what I wanted. Too bad I was nervous. At least I'd made up with Levi. I predicted Helen's next words before she said them.

"You should pack an overnight bag."

Levi wouldn't love the idea of me going away with his mom, but at least I'd just spent the night with him. It would have been worse if I'd made him suffer first.

"Okay, I will. Thanks for setting this up."

"It's not a problem, sweetie. It will be fun to spend some time away." She sounded genuinely happy about it.

"Great. Just let me know when and where to meet you."

"I will."

I hung up just as Levi came out of the bathroom. I was glad I was already off the phone. Talking to his mom while watching him in a towel would have been seriously awkward.

Even with us on good terms, Levi was really surprised when I told him my new plans. I decided breakfast was as good a time as any to break the news to him. He'd taken me to breakfast at Camellia Grill. It's a little restaurant right near campus with great breakfast food, burgers, and milk shakes. If it hadn't been eight thirty in the morning, I probably would have gotten a shake.

"You're going to see my grandma? Please tell me you're kidding." Levi took a bite of his omelet.

"It's not a big deal. Your mom and I are going for one night." I turned my stool to look at him. The only place to sit was at the counter.

"Not a big deal?" He put down his fork on his empty plate. "First you sneak over to have an afternoon coffee date with my mom, now both of you are going to visit my grandma?"

"It wasn't a coffee date. We had mimosas, and you drove me. I didn't sneak anywhere. Anyway, it's a two hour drive."

He smiled. "Just promise me I'm not in trouble. I can hardly handle you when you're mad, and my mom, forget it. The three of you scheming against me together—I can't even think about it."

"Wow, the truth comes out."

"The truth?" He put some cash down on the counter.

"You are terrified of women." It was funny watching Levi act nervously about something. Very little scared him—well, besides, the thought of me leaving him.

"I am not."

"Come on, Levi. You're freaking out about your grandma."

"See if you're still making fun of me after you meet her. I love her, she's an amazing lady, and generally I'm on her good side, but I've seen what happens to people when they make her mad."

I shuddered. "Way to freak me out before I go."

He took my hand to help me down from my stool. "I could always go with you…"

"Oh wait. I just thought of something. I need a Pteron with me, don't I? Do you think Hailey would mind coming?"

"I already offered my services."

"If you came, and I say 'if' loosely, would you promise to give us space? Maybe give us some girl time?"

"Girl time?" He laughed. "Sure, I'll hang out with my grandpa."

"Wait, he's still alive?"

"Yeah...why wouldn't he be?"

"No one mentioned him. Helen said we were just going to see Georgina."

"That's because Georgina runs everything. My grandpa just sits back and lets her do what she wants. He's enjoying retirement." Levi opened the door, and we walked out to his car.

"All right, do you want to tell your mom, or should I?"

He opened my door. "I will. Maybe she'll spill more than you."

"There's nothing to spill." I felt guilty lying, but there was no reason to upset him. Besides, I had to find out the truth.

Chapter Nine

"What is he doing here?" I pointed at the figure leaning against the side of the car that would be taking us to Georgina's. I was surprised when Levi told me we had to take a car with a driver, but supposedly his grandmother got mad when the family didn't act like 'their position required.' I gathered using a chauffeur was the appropriate mode of transportation for a royal family.

"Nice to see you too, Princess." Jared smirked.

"He was up for the trip. This way, if Grandpa falls asleep, I still have something to do."

"Great." I moved to open my door, but the driver took care of it for me before I could react. He obviously wasn't human—but he seemed even faster than a Pteron.

Since four of us were going, we were taking an SUV with three rows of seats. I moved all the way back, not wanting Helen to have to climb so far.

Levi slipped in right next to me. He reached over and buckled my seatbelt.

"Just because we're in the back seat doesn't mean you need to buckle me in."

He smiled. "I just wanted an excuse to get close."

"Because sitting right next to me isn't close enough?"

"Nope. Definitely not close enough." His lips hovered inches from mine.

"You're not going to try anything with your mom around, right? I don't have to remind you of how incredibly inappropriate that would be."

"What about in front of my grandma?" He smirked.

I shoved his arm. "Gross. Behave."

I turned to look out the window. I watched as Robert and Helen walked down their front porch. Robert said something and Helen turned to him and smiled. Despite how incredibly different their personalities were, they seemed so in love. I hoped that if Levi and I managed to pull things together and get married, we'd be that happy at their age.

"What are you thinking about?" Levi leaned over to look out the window with me.

"Your parents. Getting older. Whether we'll still be in love."

He took my hand in his. "We'll still be in love." He said it so simply but it did something to me. I looked into his eyes and there was complete conviction.

"I hope so."

"I'm just glad to hear you talking about us growing old together."

"Because you think about it all the time?"

"Not all the time…but sometimes."

"Hi, Allie. Levi." Helen ducked inside the car.

I smiled. "Hi, Helen."

My jaw about dropped when Robert sat down next to her. What was he doing?

As if he was reading my mind, he turned in his seat. "Hello, Allie. My schedule opened up, and I decided I'd make the trip to see my parents as well. I was surprised but thrilled that you were anxious to meet my mother."

I struggled to come up with a response, but Helen saved me. "Allie understands the importance of getting advice from the women who came before her. I think it's admirable."

The look Robert gave me was a combination of suspicion and 'I'm going to get you.' So much for getting on better terms with my future father-in-law. I still couldn't quite mesh this Robert with the one who got nostalgic about winning over Helen.

Thankfully, Robert turned back around in his seat. Jared got into the passenger seat, and the driver took off.

"You okay?" Levi whispered in my ear.

I nodded. I wasn't. What if Robert found out what information I was looking for? Whatever I was, I was positive Robert knew. He just didn't want me to know. That just made it more important I find out. I didn't have the energy to make conversation while Robert was listening. I went with the simplest solution. I moved Levi's arm around my shoulder and leaned my head on him, closing my eyes.

He kissed my forehead. "I guess I tired you out, huh?"

I mumbled a yes without opening my eyes. I'd spent another night with him—I promised myself I'd stay in my dorm at least a few days the next week.

Robert laughed. "I take it you two are enjoying the engagement present."

Levi stroked my hair. "Of course. It's perfect."

"Good. Allie must really want to see Georgina to give up your first weekend in the new house," Robert said with obvious sarcasm.

Levi rested his hand on my shoulder. "It doesn't matter. We'll still enjoy ourselves this weekend."

That was right. I kept thinking we'd have separate rooms, but of course not. In his family's eyes, we were already married. How in the world was I going to talk to Georgina alone?

I squeezed my eyes shut tighter. Even the comforting rhythm of Levi's heartbeat wasn't enough to relax me. I'd gotten through the week thinking I had a plan, now I was left with nothing. I couldn't give up. If it were humanly possible, I'd find a way.

**

The Laurent country house, or at least that's what they called it, was only a few hours away from New Orleans, but it might as well have been a different world. The drive up to the house took us through a spectacular alley of oaks. My eyes were glued to the window, and I appreciated how slow the driver was going so I could enjoy the view. And that was just the driveway. Surrounded by acres of land, the mansion could have come straight out of *Gone with the Wind*. The houses in the city were gorgeous, but the setting added even more to this one.

"Impressive, huh?" Jared gave me a hand to help me down from the car even though I didn't need it. I glanced around to see the reason for the unnecessary gesture and discovered it instantly. Levi was already embracing a striking woman. She was tall, with a head full of silvery gray hair. Noticing me, she pulled away from Levi.

"And this must be your Allie."

Clearly I wasn't going to correct the matriarch of the Laurent family for calling me Levi's like he owned me or something. I was going to just have to let it go.

"Hi, Mrs. Laurent. It's wonderful to meet you." I held out a hand.

She accepted the handshake, and she definitely didn't correct my formal greeting. "Pleasure." She turned to Levi. "I understand why you chose her. I'm sure she keeps you very entertained."

What? Had Levi's grandmother just hinted about our sex life?

"Justin, would you mind helping the driver with their bags?" She moved her hands flippantly at Jared.

I struggled to keep down a snicker as Jared nodded. "Yes, ma'am."

Levi shook his head. "Grandma, you know his name is Jared."

She retied a light pink sweater around her shoulders. "I can't be bothered to know the name of every Pteron in New Orleans."

If Jared was annoyed by the treatment, he didn't show it. He grabbed the bags the driver couldn't manage.

"Allie, Helen, why don't we go inside and let the men do what men do." She linked one of her arms with mine and the other with Helen's. This woman was something else.

I glanced over my shoulder to catch Levi's eye. He grinned at me and shrugged.

Georgina led us through the entry way and all the way to the back of the house. We stepped down into a sunroom.

"Sangrias for everyone," Georgina said to a male servant I didn't notice until I was already seated in a high back chair positioned to look outside. Georgina was seated next to me, with Helen on her other side. Evidently she liked to be in the middle.

No one said anything until we each had a drink. "Thank you," I said quietly as the guy who couldn't have been more than a few years older than me turned to leave.

He gave me a terse smile before leaving the sunroom and closing the doors behind him. I'm sure it wasn't fun to work for Georgina.

"Are you keeping my grandson satisfied?"

I coughed as the first sip of my sangria went down the wrong tube. That had been happening with increasing frequency lately.

"Georgina, I don't think that's an appropriate question—" Helen started.

Georgina interrupted. "Nonsense, the girl can answer."

I recovered enough to take another sip. I was going to need it. "I think so."

"You're done playing with him, then? You're done treating the future king as though he's nothing more than a boy?" Her voice was hard, rough, and icy all at once.

I wanted to disappear. She knew? "Levi and I have had our differences, but I never treated him—"

"Don't waste your breath. I know exactly what you did. I'd blame it on your age, but I was younger than you when I met Harold."

I needed to be respectful, to nod my head. That's what you're supposed to do when you need someone's help. But I couldn't. "Did Harold trick you too?"

She turned to me with a steely expression. "No. He didn't. I would never have gone to bed with a man unless I knew it was for life."

I got chills. "Excuse me? Are you implying I am somehow to blame because I chose to sleep with him?"

"I'm not implying anything. I'm saying it."

"Well, I'm saying you're wrong. What Levi did to me was horrible. I've forgiven him, I love him, but that doesn't change what he did. My reaction was normal, perfectly normal."

"I don't care what happened before. You're going to make my grandson happy, and you're going to be a proper queen." She folded her hands in her lap.

Helen put a hand on her mother-in-law's arm. "Georgina, there's no reason to be upset. That's exactly why we're here, isn't it, Allie?"

"Yes. Now that Levi and I have moved past our personal problems, I'm ready to learn more about my responsibilities."

Georgina let out a dramatic sigh. "Finally, a rational thought."

I bit my tongue to keep my mouth shut.

"You have good posture, and you hold yourself well. Who taught you that?"

"Excuse me?"

"It's a simple question. Girls of your generation do not carry themselves that way unless they've been taught."

"My mother."

"Is she from an esteemed family?"

"No, but she was a model."

"Oh, I see. Your father is the one with the money, then?"

"I don't see how my family's finances have anything to do with my role as queen?"

"Everything about you does. Being Queen of The Society isn't merely a job. It's not a line for your resume as you young people seem to say these days. Being queen is a role, a life, one that you will keep until your own son and his mate are ready to take over." She sipped her drink. I decided to hold my tongue, I assumed there was more. "Your childhood family background, their secrets, their mistakes can hurt our family—your new family."

"My dad's in business."

"Yes, I know. He purchased the Crescent City Hotel, but that doesn't tell me where the money comes from."

"It was his father's business first. He built it from the ground up."

"Where is your grandfather from?"

"He was born in New York. That whole side of my family has lived there since they came over from London in the 1800s." For once, my nerdy need to know everything about my family history was coming in handy.

"And your mother's family?"

"She's more mixed. I think—"

Georgina didn't let me finish. "Is any of her family Russian?"

"Yes. My great grandmother was from some small town. I think it's called Penza."

"Penza, really?" Her eyes widened.

"I'm guessing you've heard of it?"

"I have a friend from there, that's all." She stiffened. "Have you given any thought to what your goals will be during your reign?"

"My goals?" Currently my only goal was to get Jess away from my insane ex-boyfriend and the rest of the Blackwells.

"Yes. I worked to get women more actively involved in The Society."

"But no—" I stopped just in time. I was about to say no women were actively involved. The leadership was completely male dominated.

Georgina glared at me. "What were you about to say?"

"But no one told me I needed a platform or anything."

"I'm telling you now. Helen has been working on education—what do you plan to do?"

"Inter-family relations." I wasn't sure what I was getting at, but I worked it out as I spoke. "So many of the problems we have now could have been avoided if the major Pteron families spoke more."

"And you've reached that conclusion based on what evidence?"

"I'm sure you've heard about my high school boyfriend?"

"Yes, unfortunately." She scowled.

"If the Blackwells and Laurents had open lines of communication, we could just tell them to back off because I already belong to Levi." I wanted to cringe, but I pretended I was talking about my heart. That did belong to him.

"I hope you aren't planning to open those lines of communication yourself."

I gripped the arm of my chair. "Of course not. That's for the king to do."

Georgina smiled for the first time. "That's right. So your part would be to reach out to the women of the other families."

"Exactly, and maybe get the kids together. If they grow up friendly…"

"I like it." Helen spoke for the first time in a while. "It fits you, and I know you'll do a fantastic job with it."

"We'll see." Georgina leaned back in her chair.

"Have the major families always fought?" The more I thought about it, the more obvious the root of the problem seemed.

When Georgina didn't respond, Helen did. "No. We used to get along fine. Things fell apart about twenty years ago."

"Oh…that recently?"

Georgina abruptly changed the subject. "Helen, have you organized the trip yet?"

"The trip?" I asked, not sure I wanted to hear the answer.

"To Paris. You need clothing that suits your position."

"What's wrong with my clothes?" I looked down at my jeans and sweater. And even so, why go to Paris?

She ignored my question. "You also need to see the family estate while you're in France. You need to see our history." She turned to Helen. "On second thought, don't worry about planning the trip. I'll take her myself."

My stomach dropped. A trip to Europe with this woman sounded horrible.

Helen shifted in her seat. "Either way, it will have to wait until after the ball."

"Of course. I assume you've had her dress started?"

"It's almost done." Helen smiled.

"You aren't doing it yourself." It wasn't a question.

"I am." She held up her chin. I could tell it took some effort for Helen to stand up to Georgina. I understood completely. Georgina was intense.

"Playing around is fine, but not when it comes to her dress for this occasion. You can save that one for another time. I'll have my seamstress measure her this afternoon."

"No." I refused to hold my tongue this time. "I love the dress Helen made me. It's perfect, and Levi's going to love me in it."

I thought Georgina was going to snap at me, but I could have sworn I saw a look of actual respect cross her face. "If you're sure it will please him."

"It will."

"I'm glad to see you understand the importance of his opinion."

I nodded.

"As lovely as this chat has been, I'm going to lie down before dinner. Allie, why don't you have Levi show you the grounds? I'm sure you'll enjoy it."

Without any other warning, she got up and left. I turned to Helen. "Wow."

"Wow is right."

Chapter Ten

"How'd it go?" Levi waited for me with arms wide open as I stumbled out of the sunroom. I say stumbled because I was still somewhat shocked by the whole experience.

"Hold me."

He laughed. "Yeah, I had a hunch that might be your response. Do you want to be held here...or?"

"Georgina told me to have you show me the grounds."

He got a funny look on his face. "Yeah, let's do that."

"This isn't a trap, right?"

"A trap? Would I ever trap you?" He grinned. "Don't answer that."

I laughed. It was a testament to how much had changed that I was able to laugh at that statement. "Give me two minutes."

He must have caught me glancing around and figured out what I was looking for. "The bathroom is the third door down that hallway."

"Thanks."

I used the bathroom but lingered a moment longer to look at my reflection in the mirror. I looked different. Maybe it had been awhile since I'd really looked at myself, but I appeared older, more worn. I wondered if Levi noticed the difference. I definitely felt different—especially with how tired I'd been. Add in the headaches, and it had been a rough few weeks physically.

Levi was waiting for me outside the door. "It's going to get colder when the sun goes down." He held out my black pea coat for me.

"Thanks." I let him help me into it. I wasn't surprised that he didn't bother with his own coat. He never got cold.

"I was about to ask you if we'd be able to find our way back in the dark...stupid question."

"Not stupid, just unnecessary." He took my hand and led me down the back porch stairs.

It was twilight and there was something almost eerie about walking around the empty fields. It was a clear night, with a star filled sky that I never would have seen in the city.

Levi was right about the temperature dropping. I was grateful for my coat. I had it buttoned all the way up.

I hesitated for a moment as we neared the woods. "Is there a particular reason you're leading me into a dark forest?"

"I never took you as being afraid of the dark."

"You can't blame me for being scared of things."

His face darkened. "I'm sorry."

I hadn't meant to hurt him with my words, but the truth was, I'd had too many close calls over the past few months not to worry. "It's okay. I know I'm safe with you."

He took my hand. "There's something I want to show you."

"And it's in the woods…right. Why doesn't this surprise me?"

He laughed. "Come on."

I let him lead me deeper into the forest. I gripped his hand tightly. He might have been able to see in the dark, but I definitely couldn't. The woods were dense, with a thick cover of trees blocking out most of the light the moon and stars could have provided us. "Can't you just fly us there?"

"You want me to?"

"Yes, please." Chances were if we kept walking much longer, I'd end up with a turned ankle. No matter how coordinated you are, there's no way to avoid tripping over tree roots you can't see.

After removing his sweater and t-shirt, he wrapped his arms around me, and I enjoyed the usual feeling. The only problem was the small pellets of rain stinging my face. It hadn't been raining on the ground.

He landed, and it took me a moment to regain my balance. "Lovely weather for a walk in the woods."

"Don't worry. I'm leading us to shelter."

"Shelter?"

"You'll see." He grinned again.

I finally looked around. Right behind me was what appeared to be the mouth of a cave. "Are we going in there?"

"Yes. It's much cooler inside." He put a hand on my back.

I tentatively stepped forward, only willing to enter because of Levi's hand.

The woods seemed brightly lit compared to the complete darkness engulfing us inside the cave. I stopped moving.

"It's just a little further."

"Levi, I'm scared." I can count on my hands the number of times I've admitted that to someone.

"Don't be," he whispered in my ear as he moved us forward.

"I'll be right back." He pulled his t-shirt and sweater back on over his head. I'd assumed he was taking me inside for one reason, but maybe I'd underestimated his romantic side.

"Levi!" My chest clenched. There was no way he could leave me alone.

I blinked my eyes as the room became illuminated by several kerosene lamps. I say room, because that's what it was. I wouldn't have ever believed it was a cave.

"What is this place?" The room was furnished with a simple double bed in one corner, and a table and chairs. For all intents and purposes, it was a house.

"Check this out." I walked over to where Levi stood pointing up.

"Wow." I gaped up at what appeared to be a skylight. It provided a perfect view of the night sky. The cave must have opened up beyond the woods. "How'd you find this cave? And are you the one who fixed it up? Why isn't the rain pouring in? Is there a glass window up there?"

"It's a bit of a long story. Want to stay awhile?" He gestured to a thick rug near a fireplace I'd missed when I'd been distracted by the skylight. There were logs piled in front of it.

"Will that work?" I wasn't sure how there could be a fireplace in a cave, but then again I'd never seen a furnished cave before either.

"Absolutely."

I took a seat on the rug while Levi worked on making a fire. It didn't take long, and the warmth was almost instant. Combined with the comfortable temperature of the cave already, it was perfect. The rain had picked up outside, and distant thunder made me especially glad to be inside.

"Ready for story time?" He lay down next to me. I followed his lead, laying my head on his chest.

"I can't remember the first time I found out I was going to be king. It was always just my reality. I knew I was important, and that people went to extra lengths to do things for me."

"Not too surprising." I sat up and unbuttoned my coat, tossing it aside.

"I do remember the first time I learned about the significance of me picking a mate." He took my hand, leading me back down on the rug next to him. "I'd always thought it was the same as with other Pterons. You called the girl you married your mate, but essentially she was just your wife."

"Just your wife?" I raised an eyebrow.

"Please listen."

"Okay."

"When I was fifteen, my dad showed me the ring." He raised my hand so he could look at the rubies on my finger. "It was just like the ring Mom wore. He explained that if I gave the ring to a girl and made love to her with the right intent; it would bind us permanently—marking her as mine."

"The right intent?"

"I had to want it." He placed our entwined hands on his chest.

"So if you hadn't wanted to be with me forever…"

"Exactly. It wouldn't have worked." He played with a few strands of my hair. "I thought it was a joke. Growing up the way I did, I knew a lot of strange things existed, but a magic binding ring? Not so much." Levi paused for a second before continuing. "I laughed at Dad and told him to get a life."

"I take it that didn't go over too well?" I couldn't imagine how Robert would take getting laughed at.

"Not exactly. He sent me out here to spend the summer. Back then, my great-grandparents were still around, and they lived nearby. Dad said I couldn't come home until I accepted my position and the importance of finding the right mate."

"Oh wow, a summer with your grandparents and great-grandparents. It must have been a blast."

He laughed. "Not quite. Add in that my great-grandmother was considered crazy by some."

"Crazy?"

"Yeah, she was into magic."

"Magic?" That was a term he rarely used, and he'd just mentioned it twice. It seemed there was even more to The Society than I imagined.

"She was human, but she had some witch in her bloodlines."

"Oh…people are born witches?"

"Yes. I mean, some humans try to practice it, but there are born witches. My great-grandfather took a lot of slack for picking her, I'm sure, but I guess he really wanted her."

I smiled. All these happy couples in Levi's family. "Okay. Continue."

"My great-grandma knew why my dad sent me out here, and she told me she knew what I needed to do if I wanted to go home."

I sat up on an elbow. I was dying to hear more.

"I asked her how, and she just said to trust her. She asked to see my ring, so I gave it to her. Dad insisted I bring it with me. Part of me wanted to throw it in a river, but I knew he'd kill me if I did. She disappeared for a few hours, and when she came back she put the ring in my palm. She'd put it on a thick silver chain and just said, 'Here, wear this tonight.' Then she kissed me on the cheek and walked away."

"Weird…"

He nodded before continuing. "I decided to humor her. I don't know why, I just did. I went to bed with the ring around my neck."

I stroked his chest through his gray sweater. "What happened?"

"I had this crazy dream. I was insanely happy with a girl I didn't know. I couldn't even see her face, but I knew she was beautiful. The feeling was incredible—it was like life was perfect. There was a scene in the dream—we made love in front of the fire in a cave with a skylight open to the sky—it was picture-perfect. I woke up with this ridiculous desire to find that cave. I just knew it was real. I spent weeks exploring, and then I found it. Of course, I made a few modifications since then."

"Did you build all of this? The fireplace?" I looked around. I didn't know much about this sort of thing, but I doubted most fifteen-year-olds could have fixed it up so well.

"My grandpa is really good at carpentry and he helped me. The hardest part was the fireplace, and to answer your earlier question, yes there is a glass window in the skylight. We wouldn't want to let the rain in. If my grandpa thought it was weird that I was suddenly interested in furnishing a cave in the middle of the woods, he didn't show it."

"Is this a joke? That just doesn't sound like something you'd do at fifteen."

"It's no joke. I was on a mission. I was going to find my mate, bring her back here and find that happiness." The way he said it, the far-off look in his eyes, made me wonder just how unhappy his childhood was. "I kept the ring around my neck and searched for her. I didn't know what she looked like, but I figured I'd just know."

"I'm guessing that quest didn't last long."

"No. After a few months, I just got pissed off. Why give me that damn dream just to make it impossible? My great-grandma got sick around then, but I confronted her. She told me I needed to have the experience in order to keep myself on the right path."

"So how'd you go from searching for your mate to sleeping with anything that walked?" I tried to say it casually, but it hurt. I hated thinking about how many other girls he'd slept with—and discarded.

"I was tired of hurting. It was like a piece of me was missing. I needed to fill it—and forget. It didn't take long to realize an endless supply of girls could make it easier. After a while, the pain went away, and I moved on. That is, until I met you…"

"You just wanted to sleep with me."

"At first, sure, but I quickly realized it was more—so much more." He ran a finger over my lips. "That first time we kissed, I sensed it. And after the beach, I knew it for sure."

"You couldn't have actually thought I was that girl."

"Of course, I did. I knew it."

"How?"

"I just knew." He traced circles on my arm.

"You said in the dream we were in front of the fire."

"Yeah…I remember every detail."

"That's impossible."

"More impossible than a ring you can't take off?"

"I guess not…"

He kissed the back of my hand. "You were worth waiting for."

"Waiting for? You call what you did waiting for me?"

"I would have left. I wanted to just get the hell out of my life. I wanted to let someone else take over. I think that's what my great-grandma meant when she said it would keep me on the right path. I think part of me, even if it was small, was afraid that if I left, I'd never find the girl—you."

"This better not just be some weird trick to get me to sleep with you." I tried to laugh, but his face was completely serious.

"I love you, Allie. I know I suck at showing you sometimes, but I really do."

"Why do you think you needed to find this cave? What did it have to do with keeping you on your path?"

"You know how I said I almost left it all behind?"

I nodded.

"I was going to tell my dad when we were out here visiting. I figured it would be better to do it with my grandparents as buffers. My grandpa sensed what I was doing and dragged me out here to the cave. I still remember how he sat me down on that chair." He pointed to one of the four situated around the table. "He said, 'I was with you when you worked on this cave—don't you think your mate deserves a chance to come here at least once?'"

"How bad was your childhood?" I had to know. What was so bad that he almost left?

"My dad is what he is. I was never good enough, and he never let me forget it. I was his greatest disappointment in life."

"Levi, that's not true." I put a hand on his arm.

"It is. The first time in my life he said he was proud of me was when I told him I'd found you and made you my mate."

"But I'd run away…"

"Yeah…"

"We both have daddy issues."

"Daddy issues?"

"Come on, you know what I mean." I put my head back down.

"He worked a lot, right?" He stroked my hair.

"Yeah. My parents were divorced when I was so little that I didn't know any different, but as the years went on, he visited less and less. The only good thing was that when we were together, he always made me feel like his little princess."

"Princess, eh?"

"Don't—"

"Go on."

"I was never as important as his work though. I don't just mean the hours. Dad's company doesn't only buy hotels, they also buy other places. One time, when I was seven, they bought this old amusement park. I was with

Dad when he went to look at a carousel they were taking apart to sell the pieces. It was one of those really old wooden ones. I fell in love with one of the animals. It was a flamingo that was a double-seater. I don't know why I loved it—maybe it was the wings."

"You've always liked wings, huh?" He arched an eyebrow.

"Levi." I rolled my eyes. "As I was saying. I loved it. I thought Dad was going to get it for me...my birthday was coming up. I remember seeing the drop cloth in the living room that was obviously covering something big. I just knew it was the flamingo."

"But it wasn't?"

"Nope. It was a horse from a much newer carousel, or even one that'd just been made in a factory or something. Dad saw my face fall and asked why I didn't like the horse. It had a purple saddle, and I loved purple. I asked why he didn't get me the one I wanted."

"Did he tell you why?"

"The biggest stockholder saw it when it was unloaded at his office. He wanted it for his daughter. Dad gave it away and figured he could just give me the horse instead." I fidgeted. "I was so angry, I pushed over the horse and some of the paint chipped. I told him to get the stupid thing out of my sight. He looked devastated, so I ran. He never said anything about it, but he never brought me on any of his work trips again. Oh my god, this is embarrassing. I sound like a spoiled brat."

"You don't sound like anything. You were an eight-year-old whose dad broke her heart."

"So yeah, we both have daddy issues."

"I guess so. Let's hope our kids don't have them."

"Or mommy issues."

He laughed. "All right, neither."

"We're really going to have kids one day, huh?"

"Don't you want to have kids?" He looked at me seriously.

"In theory…"

"Same here. Let's agree to not bring that topic up again until you're done with college."

"Good deal." I snuggled into his side.

"Don't move. I just want to check the fire."

I waited as he stoked the flames. He also took the quilt off the bed. "I promise this hasn't been sitting here for seven years."

"You've been back recently?"

"I was here this summer…"

He laid the quilt down right next to me. I moved onto it and he joined me.

I slipped my hand under his sweater and t-shirt. "Do you think this is going to live up to your dream?"

"I have a hunch it'll be better. Reality has to be better."

"I love you." I leaned over and kissed him. So often he was the instigator, but I needed my lips against his.

"I love you more than anything." He brushed my hair back from my face. "More than anything."

I pushed his sweater over his head, following up with his t-shirt. "I could look at you for hours."

"Only hours? I could stare at you for days." He pulled off my sweater. "Or maybe years." He unclasped my bra.

"The problem is I need you to do more than stare."

He grinned. "So do I, Al. So do I."

He cupped each of my breasts and returned his lips to mine. Normally by this point, he'd be trying to get me out of my pants, but he was taking it a little slower. I liked it.

"You're wearing light green panties."

"How'd you know?"

"I've dreamed this before."

"You remember the color of my underwear?"

"It's still me, Al. It might have been an emotional dream, but I'd still remember a detail like that. You never wear green panties."

"I haven't done laundry since we got back."

"Likely story." He moved his mouth down to my breast, and I moaned.

I struggled a moment with his buckle, but eventually I got it and unzipped his pants.

He moved his mouth. "In a hurry?"

"I want you."

"Really? I'd have had no idea." He shifted to slide out of his khakis and boxers. "But the question is whether I'm ready for you." He ran a hand down my stomach, stopping at the button of my jeans.

"You're ready."

"I love when you boss me around, babe."

"Then you're going to enjoy life with me."

"Yeah, I think so too." He finally unbuttoned my jeans and pulled them down. He slipped off my panties. "When did you realize you loved me?"

"I didn't admit it to myself right away, but it was that night at Antoine's. As weird as it felt to have you giving me a ring so early, a part of me actually looked forward to getting an engagement ring from you."

"I guess I gave you what you wanted."

I laughed. "I guess so. But how about giving me what I want now?"

"And what's that?"

"You."

"At your service." Once he started, my whole world spun. It was so much more intense than usual. It was perfect—or beyond perfect, and I knew I'd never be whole without him. If saving Jess meant leaving Levi, it also meant losing a part of myself I was positive I could never get back.

"I'm yours." The words came out as a moan.

"I'm yours too." He kissed me, and we spent the rest of the night in front of that roaring fire, watching the starlit sky through the only cave skylight I've ever seen.

Chapter Eleven

"Keeping my boy up all night, huh?" Jared took a seat next to me at the breakfast table. We were the only ones there. I wasn't sure what the Laurent clan was up to, but I had a feeling it had something to do with me.

"Like you don't know every detail? I saw you guys talking before I went up to take a shower."

"He didn't tell me anything. He said it was an amazing night that's going to stay between you and him."

I smiled. I couldn't help it.

"I take it you found it amazing too? Sometimes you guys act like an old married couple, but other times you act like you just met—all giddy over sneaking away together or something."

"Which time is it now?"

"Both." He poured syrup on his pancakes.

The breakfast spread was seriously impressive. I'd initially only planned to have some fruit and yogurt, but when the server offered to make me a Belgian waffle, I couldn't resist.

"How is that even possible?" I spread my napkin on my lap.

He shrugged. "How would I know? I'm just the innocent bystander."

"Here's your waffle, miss." The same server set it down in front of me.

"Thanks so much."

"Would you like some whipped cream?" he asked.

"Yes, that would be great." I didn't look up as I answered. I expected Jared to be ready with a snarky comment.

Jared only smiled before diving back into his pancakes. I took it as my opportunity to move the conversation onto him.

"One day you're going to fall in love, and I hope I'm around to see it." I took a bite of my waffle. I'd made the right decision with the whipped cream.

"Are you planning on going somewhere?"

"No, but I might be really old by then."

"Oh, Princess, you're such a joy to be around in the morning."

"She is even more of a joy when she just wakes up." Levi slid into the seat next to me. "Sorry that took so long." He picked up a fork and took a bite of my waffle.

"You can get your own food."

"Be glad I'm not feeding you," he teased. I didn't want to remember how I'd had to put up with him feeding me an entire meal once at a Society event.

"Are you going to tell me what you and the rest of your family have been up to?"

"We've been talking about you." He took another bite of my waffle. I was about to argue that he shouldn't have taken a piece coated in whipped cream when he put it in my mouth instead of his own.

"Mmm, that's so good."

He leaned over to whisper in my ear. "You really like whipped cream. I need to remember that."

I nudged him. "What have you been saying about me?"

"Relax, love. We were just making plans for the day."

"Plans?"

"You're going with Grandma to see her seamstress."

"Is your mom going?"

"No. She wasn't invited."

"Oh, why not?" I needed time alone with Georgina, but I hoped Helen didn't mind.

"Because my grandmother thinks you two need alone time."

"When am I going?" I was both anxious and nervous. I hoped I could handle Georgina on my own.

"As soon as you're done here."

"Has she eaten yet?"

"Hours ago. They were making bets on whether we'd be back for lunch." He grinned.

"On that note, I'm going to get ready." I leaned over and kissed him on the cheek. "Wait, what Pterons are going with us?"

"A few of the guys that work here."

"Oh...okay." I took a final bite of my waffle, savoring the sweet taste.

"I'll meet you back down here in ten minutes." I leaned over and kissed Levi. "See ya, Jared." I waved as I headed back upstairs to grab my purse. I needed to mentally prepare myself for more time with Georgina.

***

I waited on the porch with Levi and Georgina. It was an awkward few minutes, but I knew things were probably going to get a lot more awkward once Levi wasn't around to act as a buffer. I was about to take a seat on an uncomfortable looking chair when a limo slowly pulled up to the front of the house. Apparently, we were taking an even fancier vehicle on this trip.

"Have a lovely day, Levi." Georgina embraced Levi before heading down off the porch. "Come along, Allie. We have things to do." Georgina didn't turn to wait for me.

"Have fun." Levi kissed me on the cheek before I followed Georgina down. I turned and waved at him before sliding into my seat. I was positive the 'have fun' comment was sarcastic.

The last time I'd been in a limo was for prom. I thought it was a little over the top for a trip into town to see a seamstress, but I kept that thought to myself. I straightened out my black pencil skirt, making sure it fell correctly over my thigh high boots. I hoped I looked presentable enough. Georgina certainly hadn't been a fan of the jeans look I'd gone with the day before.

We'd barely made it out of the long, winding driveway when Georgina called to the Pteron driving. "There's been a change of plans. Take us to the late Mrs. Laurent's bungalow."

"Yes, ma'am."

I looked at Georgina with shock.

She gave me a warning glance that shut me up while she hit the button for the privacy shield.

As soon as it was in place, she turned to me. "This divider is Pteron hearing proof, but we still need to be careful."

"What's going on?"

"You don't think I know why you're here? You want to know how it's possible to have attracted two different Pterons so young."

I sat up straighter. "Do you know why?"

"I think so, but I need more information. I needed to get you away from everyone."

"So you're going to help me?"

She leaned over and looked me straight in the eye. "I'll help you, but only because I know you're going to make the right decision. You will not hurt my grandson or this family."

I nodded.

"Is your grandmother still alive?"

"My mom's mom?" I remembered how interested Georgina had been in Mom's family.

"Yes. Is she?"

"No. She passed away when I was a sophomore in high school."

Georgina straightened her hair with her hand. "That makes this trickier, but I think we can figure it out on our own."

"Is there something that can help us at your mother-in-law's?"

"Yes, several things."

"Okay." I settled back against my seat. This was exactly what I'd been hoping for, but I was still terrified.

"Did you like your tour of the grounds last night?" She suddenly changed the topic. I was sure she knew exactly where Levi had taken me.

"Yes. It was informative and romantic."

"It is romantic, isn't it? He waited seven years to meet the literal girl of his dreams."

"Even if I was twelve when he had the dream…" I mumbled.

"It was a dream of the future…you were eighteen." She opened her purse, searching through it for something.

"I know. You should have seen how his eyes lit up when he told me about it."

"He'd been waiting a long time to see that dream actually occur…" She pulled out a hard candy, unwrapping it carefully before she put it in her mouth. She didn't offer me one.

"It sounds like you've been talking about this more recently than when he was fifteen."

"He came to see me in August. You weren't speaking to him unless you had to, and he was beside himself."

"Really? He came to you about it?" I didn't bother to hide my surprise. I couldn't imagine Levi going to his grandmother for girl advice.

"I think he wanted to come back to the cave…"

I fidgeted with my skirt. "He mentioned he did come back to see it."

"He asked me whether it was possible that he could have messed up so badly that now the dream wouldn't happen."

"Why was he so fixated on the dream—on one particular night?"

She bit into the candy, making a cracking sound. "It wasn't the night, but what it symbolized."

"Just that it symbolized we were together?"

"Just? How is that 'just' anything? The bond between a royal Pteron and his mate is stronger than any other."

"I know." I did. What Levi and I had was intense, so intense it scared me.

We sat in silence for the rest of the thirty-five minute drive. The telltale throbbing started, and I knew I was in for another headache. Hopefully, I'd get back to Levi before it got too bad. I still hadn't mentioned the headaches to him. He'd probably overreact, or if he found out he made them better, he'd want us glued together.

The limo pulled up out front of a beautiful house that certainly didn't look like a bungalow. Georgina instructed the driver and his partner to wait for us outside. They went in first to check the house and then left.

The entryway was simple, but the living room it opened up into was anything but. Crown molding, wood floors, and tall arched ceilings were a few highlights from the formal room.

Georgina gestured for me to sit in a plush armchair. "Coffee, tea, brandy?"

"Brandy? It's ten a.m."

"So? You may need something strong for this talk."

"Brandy, then." I don't know why I said yes. I hated drinking straight liquor.

She poured two glasses and took a seat on a chair across from me before pulling a worn book off the shelf.

"Do you come here a lot?" It dawned on me how strange it was that the house still felt lived in if the owner died seven years before. The furniture was neat and uncovered, and the wood floors were spotless.

She smiled. "I like to get away every once in a while."

I didn't press it further. There was no reason to. "What's that book?"

"It's a Pteron history book." She brushed a layer of dust off the velvety black cover. Evidently the book hadn't been used in a while.

"There are books about Pteron history?"

"Of course. Why wouldn't there be?"

I shifted in my chair, trying to get more comfortable. "Isn't it all secretive?"

"These books aren't easy to come by."

"I'd imagine."

"How much do you understand about how the royal lines work?" She set down the book on her lap.

"I know there are a few ranking families but that the Laurents have been in charge of the American region for a long time."

"You're correct. We've been in power for generations. That's generally how it works. The only way the line usually changes is if the first born son fails to mate and have an heir."

"Usually? I thought that was the only way."

Georgina opened the book and flipped through the pages.

"Here, read this." She handed me the heavy book.

"*The Enchantress*?" I read the fancy script title at the top of the page.

"Yes. That section." She leaned back in her chair. "Read it aloud."

"*Every few generations, there have been changes in lines that deviate from the usual failure to bear an heir. In each case, a human woman has been the cause.*" I left my finger on the spot I was on. "How could a human change anything?"

"Keep reading."

"This woman is said to attract the male heir of each line in a way that cannot be denied. Whoever this woman chooses will become the new king. Three of the great Pteron wars can be traced back to such a woman. She is called an enchantress even though she is purely human."

I felt sick. "You think I'm one of these?"

"I don't see any other explanation."

"So that means." I didn't want to say it. "So Levi's only with me because of this weird Pteron lust?"

"Of course not!" Georgina was out of her chair before I could process it. She bent down over me. "No. He loves you. Don't confuse attraction with love. He may have first been attracted to you because of what you are, but that doesn't change the deeper feelings he has. He's been in love with you for years."

"No, he hasn't. He had a dream. He was in love with the idea of me." I should have been more concerned with the revelation that I was actually some sort of Pteron magnet, but all I could think about was Levi's feelings for me.

"That's not true. If you look deep into yourself, you'll realize that." She patted my shoulder and sat back down.

"But this doesn't fit. I already picked Levi. Why is it still an issue?"

"I wondered that myself, until I found this." She pulled a smaller book from her purse. "This is my Pteron history book."

I took the book and turned to the page she had marked with a red ruby tasseled bookmark. *"Once the enchantress has accepted a ring and lays with the chosen heir, the others will no longer feel the pull, and order will be restored."*

"How does this help?"

"Were you really choosing Levi as the next king?"

"No...but I did accept the ring."

"I know that." She leaned forward. "Think about it though. Did you accept the ring knowing you were choosing him as the next king?"

My head started to spin, and I readied myself for the headache I knew was coming.

"I've been researching this since I found out about your past boyfriend. It seems this was far more common years ago but not in modern history. I have a two-part theory about this."

"What is it?" I braced myself on the arm of the chair.

"The first part is that in modern society, the families are more spread out. Five hundred years ago, the Pteron heirs would have interacted with the same human women. Now they barely speak..."

"So you're saying if I'd only met one Pteron heir, we never would have known I was anything different..."

"Exactly."

"So it was just random chance..."

Georgina paled.

"What is it?"

"This does not leave the room." She sat back in her seat, closing her eyes for a moment.

"Of course."

"That's not good enough. I need you to swear."

"To swear? Is that really necessary?" How serious was this?

She nodded.

"I swear I won't tell."

She let out a deep breath. "It wasn't random."

"How do you know?"

"I don't believe in chance encounters. There's fate, and then there's man-made interference."

"Which one is this?"

"A little of both."

I sipped my brandy. It tasted as awful as I expected.

"Robert knew about Levi's dream. He's the one who told Carol to perform the dream spell."

"Carol? Levi's great-grandmother?"

"Yes."

"He said it was for Levi's own good, but I think he wanted to make sure Levi would take a mate. He was terrified our period of rule was coming to an end. I think that's why he was always so hard on Levi…"

I tried to swallow a lump in my throat.

"I have one more passage to show you. Turn to the next page."

I hesitantly turned the page. *The heads of family are often the first to sense the enchantress. An heir must see her face-to-face to trigger the response.*

"This brings me to my second theory."

It came to me suddenly. "Back then, the fathers would have sensed it and watched who the other heirs were with."

"Exactly."

"Are you suggesting…do you think Robert knew?"

"A little over a year ago, Robert came out here to talk to his father. He was panicked. I wasn't privy to the conversation, but from what I gathered, it had to do with Levi finding the right mate."

"But how could Robert have figured out it was me?"

"I need to ask a question, and I want an honest answer."

"Okay." She was telling me way more than I expected. I'd tell her anything she needed to know.

"When did you first sleep with your high school boyfriend?"

"On our six month anniversary. We were only together a year… It was fall of my senior year."

"Right when Robert came here…"

"But how could…"

"He has spies. They must have known."

"But something about all of this is bothering me. How do we know Toby is an heir? He just said his mother's maiden name. Levi didn't recognize his name. Wouldn't Levi have known who Toby was?"

"Not if the Blackwells were trying to hide his identity…usually the line passes through a son—"

"But if there was no son…and Robert figured it out."

"He must have. What made you first come down to New Orleans?" She gripped the arm of her chair.

"My dad bought the hotel, and I came down to work for him."

"Do you know why he bought it? Did he usually buy urban real estate?"

"He owns a lot of hotels…but most of them are more the resort style." Then it hit me. "Did Robert have something to do with him buying it?"

"I don't know, but I wouldn't be surprised. He needed you to meet Levi before things went too far with Toby. He must have been afraid Toby was ready to take it to the next step."

"The next step? That's what Toby meant…"

"What? What he meant?"

I let out a deep breath. "Why are you helping me with this?"

"Isn't it obvious?"

"Not really. Doesn't this go against helping your son?"

"On the contrary, it's the only way we can fix things. We have to figure out a way to make your mating with Levi permanent—to make it impossible for you to choose another."

"Toby was at the New Year's party."

"Does Levi know?" Her eyes were locked on mine.

"Toby said he'd hurt Jess if I told…"

"That's the friend of yours who the Blackwell's have?"

"Yes. It's all my fault." I hung my head.

"No, it's not. This isn't the time to feel sorry for yourself. What happened when he saw you?"

"He told me how much he wanted me. I asked him when he'd planned to tell me about what he was." I looked down at my hand and touched my ring. "He said he would have done it on our wedding night when I accepted his ring."

"Toby knew. Damn it. Robert messed it all up by not telling Levi—by not trusting his own son."

"If Levi knew I had to agree, he would have made sure I knew what I was doing. He would have moved slower—been careful." Robert really did cause this whole mess. "So how do we fix it? They're not going to leave my friends or me alone until this is over, are they?"

"I don't know. I think you're the only one who can figure it out."

"Why?"

"Because the mistake was not giving you the choice. This is all about you."

"So what now?"

"We drink more brandy."

I let out a surprised noise. "But what about Jess?"

"Did Toby give you any idea of when you'd see him again?"

"No."

"This goes against every grain in my body as a Laurent—but I only see one option."

"What is it?"

"Call him. Tell him what he wants to hear. Maybe he knows more than we do. You attract more bees with honey, so to speak."

My jaw dropped. "Are you suggesting I flirt with him to get him to open up to me about it?"

"That's exactly what I'm suggesting."

"But—"

"That's just my advice. I don't like it, but I don't have any other brilliant ideas."

A thought suddenly occurred to me. "Why did you ask about where my grandmother's family was from?"

"Everything about enchantresses I can find seems to lead back to Russia…for whatever that's worth."

"Oh. That's strange." Then something else occurred to me. "This might be a silly question, but what are we going to tell everyone about my appointment with the seamstress?"

"What are your measurements?"

"Wait, are you going to order clothes for me?"

"Sure, it's easy enough."

"You're definitely not what I expected."

"You're exactly what I expected." She finished off her glass and set it down next to her.

"Is that good or bad?"

"Good. You're as perfect for Levi as I thought."

"So was that all an act? Being mean?"

"Of course. If I acted like I approved, they never would have agreed to let us spend today together. Levi was convinced all I needed was time with you to realize how amazing you are."

"He said that?"

"Don't act surprised, you know as well as I do how in love with you he is."

"As in love as I am…" I hoped it was true, and he did really love me. With everything else, I couldn't handle a broken heart.

***

"Finally." Levi met us at the door of the limo. His father was right next to him. He helped me out, and I needed it. By the third glass, I decided the brandy didn't taste so bad. Georgina said getting drunk was essential. That way they couldn't grill us with questions.

"Hey, Levi!" I put my arms around his neck.

"Hi, Allie. Are you drunk?"

"Very."

He glanced over my head. "How much brandy did you give her?"

"The same amount I had." Somehow Georgina didn't seem drunk.

"I liked it. I should get that more often."

"All right, time to get ready for bed, love. Let's head upstairs."

"But I'm hungry."

"Didn't you guys eat?" He brushed some hair away from my face.

"Nope. Not a thing."

"What do you want?"

"Whipped cream." I laughed.

"On second thought, are you up for a flight?"

"Why?"

"I wouldn't mind another night in the cave."

"Ohhh, yes! Let's do that."

He laughed. "Let's grab you something from the kitchen and then we'll go."

"Perfect."

"You're perfect." He kissed me gently.

"You really love me, don't you?" There was only one answer to that question I could handle hearing. I hated that I even had to doubt it now. It had been the one secure thing I had in all the craziness of my life.

"Of course. Why would you even ask that?"

"I couldn't stand it if you didn't."

He leaned in to whisper in my ear. "New goal of the night—spend all of it making sure you never question my feelings for you again."

"And food. I need food."

"I got that the first time." He led me into the kitchen. Instead of giving me whipped cream, Levi made me a grilled cheese sandwich. I'm not sure how he guessed—but it completely hit the spot. I finished my sandwich and a couple glasses of water before we walked out onto the back porch. I settled down on a couch, and I must have fallen asleep. The next thing I knew, I was curled up in Levi's arms in the little bed in the cave.

I snuggled in closer to him. I was wearing just my tank top and underwear. He'd taken off my sweater and skirt. Levi was wearing nothing but his boxers. No surprise there. "Sorry I fell asleep."

"No sorry. It's nice having you here with me. "

"I can't think of a single place I'd rather be." I closed my eyes again and let sleep take me back under.

Chapter Twelve

"Tell me everything." Hailey yanked open the door before I could turn the lock.

"Hello to you, too."

"Did Georgina know anything?"

"Yes, but you need to sit down for this, and so do I." I hung up my coat and put my boots up in my closet. I hated leaving things out.

"You have to be the slowest person in the universe."

"Or you're incredibly impatient." Really I was just trying to build up the nerve to spill out the story. I wasn't exactly proud of being an enchantress. Essentially, it meant I was a Pteron sex magnet.

"Come on, spill." Hailey took a seat on my bed.

I let out a deep breath and sat down next to her. "I need to tell you something I don't want getting back to Levi."

She grinned. "I'm good at keeping things from Levi."

I took a few more seconds to ready myself and then spilled it out. "We think I'm something called an

109

enchantress. Long story short—I attract all the possible heirs and theoretically have the power to choose the next king."

"How is that even possible? The line continues unless there's no heir."

"Supposedly, some women can change things, and evidently I'm one of them."

"So what happens?"

"Theoretically, it should be over. I have Levi's ring, but I think he messed it all up by tricking me into it. He didn't give me a choice so I didn't officially pick him."

Hailey gasped. "That idiot."

"We have to figure out a way to redo it, or make it more permanent. Until then, the Blackwells, and technically any other royal line family, could keep trying to mess with me." I'd just put two and two together and realized there were probably other heirs I needed to stay away from.

"So what's next? What do we do?"

"Georgina told me to look inside myself or flirt information out of Toby."

"What? That's an interesting set of choices."

I laughed. "I know. I'm looking inside without luck, but flirting with Toby sounds harder."

"Are you going to call him?"

"I want to, but I don't know what to say. He's going to know I'm faking."

"Text him."

"How do you flirt through text?" I pulled my knees up to my chest.

"I'm not sure, but I know someone who would." Hailey got up and disappeared into the hallway. I wasn't shocked at all when she returned with Anne.

"What's up?" Anne was as bubbly as usual. "How was your weekend?"

I thought about my response for a moment. "Interesting."

Anne put a hand in the pocket of her pink sweats. She was the kind of girl who could pull off bright colored pants. "Good interesting? Bad interesting?"

Hailey didn't give me a chance to respond. "We need your help."

Anne perked up even more. "What kind of help?"

"Can I help too?" Tiffany walked in with an English poetry book in her hand. Hailey must have interrupted her reading when she came in for Anne.

"Sure, but close the door," Hailey said quickly.

Tiffany closed and locked it.

"We need you to text dirty with Allie's ex." Hailey just blurted it out to Anne.

Anne laughed. "First of all, why? And second of all, why me?"

Hailey removed her hair clip and shook out her hair. "The second part is obvious. The first doesn't matter. We need information."

Anne seemed less excited. "I'm guessing Levi doesn't know about this?"

"Since when are you concerned about Levi?" Hailey asked.

"I'm not, but I just wanted to make sure…" Anne looked at me as she answered.

"Do you mind helping? I know it's weird." I pulled a sleeve of my sweater over my hand.

Anne grinned. "This is going to be fun, but you're going to still have to help."

I opened my contact list and clicked on Toby. Our breakup hadn't been the type where we deleted each other's number, at least not on my end. I handed Anne my phone, and everyone huddled around to watch.

Hey.

This is a surprise.

I was just thinking about you.

Oh?

Thinking about what it used to be like.

I thought you were over me.

How could I ever be over you—or your body?

"Anne!" I shrieked.

"What? I thought I was supposed to be making this dirty?"

"I can't handle this." I buried my head in my hands.

"She can stop…is this really necessary?" Tiffany put a hand on my back. I made myself continue to watch Anne type.

Are you messing with me? I warn you that would be one hell of a mistake.

I'm not messing with you. I just wanted to tell you I missed you—us.

You know I miss you. I want you so bad it hurts. You don't want to know what I'd do to have you here with me.

Does that mean you're alone?

Yes it does. Are you?

Yes. If I wasn't I couldn't be doing what I'm doing.

"Anne! Stop! Stop!" I clenched my comforter to stop myself from grabbing the phone.

What are you doing? I wonder if it's what I'm about to do.

Anne looked at me. "What answers do you need?"

I scrunched my eyes closed. "I need to know how it would work. How I could choose him. I think he knows."

"Choose him?" Tiffany asked.

"It's complicated."

"I have to act now. I think I know how to do this." Anne got all serious like she was about to work through some massive equation or something.

Let's play a game.

A game? I'm beginning to wonder if it's really you.

"Damn it. Tell me something only you guys would know. Make it personal," Anne said impatiently.

"Do I have to?"

"Yes!" Anne snapped.

"We used to hook up in his old tree house when his dad was home."

"Perfect."

Who else would it be? You know what I dreamed about last night?

What?

Your tree house.

Yeah? What about it?

Can we play the game?

Will I like this game?

I proved it was me. Prove it's you.

You like having sex when you know you might get caught.

All three of my friends turned to stare at me.

I'm sure I was beet red. I wasn't sure if it was possible to feel more embarrassed. "It's him... obviously."

Ready for my game?

Yes.

Let's preview what our next time together is going to be like.

So you've made up your mind? You want to come back to me?

There was something so hopeless about that text, it ate at me.

If you make it enticing enough.

I will, but this is boring.

Boring? I grabbed my phone from Anne. *I'm boring?*

I don't want to see your words. I need to hear your voice...or even better see you. Can you skype?

Anne took the phone. *No skype. I don't want to get off my bed.*

Call me. I need to hear you.

"I can't call him! It's okay when you are doing it, but I can't do this. It feels like I'm cheating on Levi."

"I can't fake your voice..." Anne looked at me.

"What should I do?" I glanced at Hailey.

"Either we find another way or you talk to him."

"I'd be a pretty selfish friend if I didn't try. Jess needs me to do this." My stomach was in knots, but I was out of options. Until I fixed the bond with Levi, the Blackwells weren't going to give up.

I took the phone from Anne and pressed call.

"Hey, baby." Did he have to call me that?

"Hi."

"So where'd this all come from? Last time I saw you, you were still trying to get rid of me."

"I told you. I was just reminiscing."

"I do that constantly. I can't get you out of my head. I replay our time together on repeat. I remember what every inch of you feels like, tastes like. And that kiss in the hot tub. It was hot. If you'd only let it go where it wanted to go..."

Hailey gave me a funny look. She could hear every word. I hadn't told her about the kiss.

"I wasn't ready."

"You're ready now?" His voice was so hopeful. It didn't sound evil like the kidnapper he was.

"How would it even work?" Maybe I could get it out of him without any sex talk.

"Weren't we supposed to be playing a game?"

"You're the one who wanted to hear my voice."

"And we can't play that kind of game talking? It wouldn't be the first time…"

I cringed. Hailey could hear, and the look on her face was not one I wanted to see.

"I'm scared." That was somewhat honest.

"You're never scared."

"I am right now."

"Why'd you text me?"

"I wanted to talk."

"I want to believe you, but not with the way you're acting." He paused. "Is he with you?"

"You think I'd be talking to you with Levi here?"

"Don't say his name!" Toby grumbled.

"Okay…"

"You're not his. You're mine."

"If it helps, he wasn't very happy to discover he wasn't my first Pteron."

"No, he wasn't your first. I was. I was your first everything… I was first, and I'll be your last. We'll just have to forget about the little blip in-between."

"How is it possible? Please tell me."

"Not yet. I'd rather show you when the time comes"

"But—if you tell me now, I'll be more likely to come."

"Save it, Allie. You suck at this. Trying to bargain kind of kills the seduction angle. It doesn't matter. I'll take care of everything."

"What am I supposed to do?"

"You're going to come with me when I tell you it's time. You're going to choose me, and we'll leave all this bullshit behind us. I should be so damn mad at you right now, but I still just want you. Do you know how hard this is?"

"But none of it's real. It's just Pteron lust or whatever. You don't love me. Just block it out."

He laughed dryly. "So you know what you are?"

"Yes."

"You're like a drug, and I've been in a constant state of withdrawal since I last had you. I shouldn't have waited. I should have just given you my ring. I wanted to give you time, do it right."

"Are you really the Blackwell heir? How didn't Le- he know?"

"My grandfather tried to keep it a secret, but yes, I'm the heir."

"For what it's worth, I'm sorry you're hurting, but you need to let Jess go."

"You're sorry? If you were sorry, you'd have come back to me sooner. If you were sorry, you would have given me what I needed when I saw you. You're not sorry, but it's okay. I know you love me, and I want us enough for both of us. I'll remind you of how good we are together. It's only going to take one night. One night of being with me as I really am and you'll forget all about him. I'm stronger than him, I have more to give. I'll make you feel ten times better than he ever could. You won't be able to walk after a night with me transformed."

116

"Is that supposed to be a good thing?"

"What part?"

"The not being able to walk after a night with you?"

Anne started cracking up.

"Is someone with you?"

"No…"

"Wait a second. It wasn't even you texting me, was it? Damn it, Allie."

"Toby—"

"And for the record, it is a good thing. If you can't imagine that then clearly you haven't had the right Pteron experience yet."

"Ugh." I hung up and threw my phone.

"I don't even know where to start." Hailey got up and started pacing around the room.

"Hmm, let's start with how she likes to have sex when she knows she might get caught." Anne laughed.

"None of this is funny!" I wrung my hands.

Hailey tried to hide a smile but failed miserably. "That part is. I so never imagined you were like that. Does Levi know that's a turn on?"

"It's not. I don't need that kind of thing with Levi."

Anne raised an eyebrow. "Ohhhh. Levi's good enough that you don't need to ratchet up the heat to get off?"

"Stop it, both of you!"

"I don't think that's really you," Tiffany said softly.

"Thanks. I appreciate someone coming to my defense."

"I mean, so much of this is supernatural." She folded her hands in her lap. "I don't get all the details, but it sounds like there's something about you that attracts these Pterons and you're supposed to figure out which one to choose?"

"Yes. To choose the next king."

"Then it's going to be affecting your body. The needing more with Toby was probably the supernatural power's way of telling you he wasn't the right one..."

I smiled. "You're right. You're right. Oh my god, I think you're a genius. I just have to find a way to let that supernatural power know I already picked Levi."

"You guys do realize how ridiculous this sounds, right?" Anne asked.

"Yes, but I'm kind of ready to accept it."

Anne stood up. "So what now? What's our plan?"

"I have no clue. We wait for Toby and come up with a way to get Jess."

"Without losing you..." Hailey had stopped laughing.

"Let's hope."

"No hoping. You're not going to the Blackwells. Put aside personal issues, you just admitted that you know Levi is the right choice. Going to Toby could seriously mess things up for The Society. You have to have this power for a reason." Hailey was probably right, but she was also extremely biased.

"You're right. I just need to get some fresh air. Anyone want to go for a walk in Audubon Park?"

"Sure. Let me get a coat," Tiffany offered.

"I'll come." Hailey slipped on sneakers.

"You don't have to."

"I kind of do, but I want to anyway."

"You sure? Maybe once we figure this out, you'll be done babysitting."

"I'm not babysitting, we both know that."

"I feel gross." Images of Levi's face swam through my mind. If he only knew what I'd been doing.

"You didn't do anything wrong. You couldn't even flirt with Toby. Take it as a sign that you are definitely ready for a monogamous relationship with Levi." Anne opened the door.

"Yeah...a monogamous, never-ending relationship."

Chapter Thirteen

"Hey, it's me. When you finish your meeting, can you meet me at the house? I love you." I left my third voicemail on Levi's phone. I usually wasn't like that. I left one and waited, but I needed to see him. Talking to Toby had messed with me. Even a walk in the park didn't help. We'd all come back to the new house, but everyone left because I made them. I knew there was a Pteron watching from outside, but I at least felt like I was alone. My head pounded and all I wanted to do was curl up with Levi. I hated feeling so needy. It wasn't a feeling I was used to, and it wasn't one I liked.

My life was a mess. I'd known it for months but it was only getting worse. I shouldn't have been feeling bad for myself considering Jess was being held captive, but I couldn't help it. I felt useless. All I wanted to do was find her. I'd have done it by myself if I thought it were remotely possible. I would have traded places with her, if I thought it was that simple. I just had this ugly feeling that she knew too much. Something might happen to her once they got me. What if she became expendable? I had to use my head, but I didn't even know what to think anymore.

My phone buzzed, and I grabbed it. The text had to be from Levi. It wasn't.

When you're done being someone's plaything, I'm here. I didn't mean to leave things like that. I love you, baby. Don't forget it over the next few weeks. After that, I'll show you every day.

A few weeks? Is that all the time I had? I turned over my phone. I couldn't even handle seeing his name on the screen. If it came down to getting back with Toby or letting Jess die, I knew what the answer would be. It didn't matter that every inch of me rebelled against the thought of anyone but Levi touching me ever again.

I tried to distract myself. I took a bath, using the lilac bubble bath I found under the sink. Twenty minutes later, I got out and tried Levi again. Nothing. What could possibly be more important than making sure I was okay after I left four messages? The only person he wouldn't leave a meeting with was his dad. Then a horrible thought hit me. What if his dad told him what I was, and he was angry for falling for me—angry that it wasn't real love.

I lay down on the bed without bothering to get dressed. It didn't seem worth the effort. I felt horrible.

I was fading in and out of sleep when I heard the front door open. I got up, not caring that I was wearing just a towel.

"You're not Levi." My heart sunk. I needed him.

"No, sorry to disappoint you, Princess."

"Where is he, Jared?" I pulled the towel tighter around me.

"With his dad. Where else would he be?" Jared tried to avert his eyes. I'm sure I was making him uncomfortable.

"Did he send you?"

"Yeah. He got a message out to me."

"Oh." I sat down on the landing with my feet on the next step. "Will he be out soon?"

"You guys have eight o'clock reservations at Brennan's."

"We're going out?"

Jared studied some spot on the wall several feet above me. "Yeah…I think he wanted to surprise you."

"Oh…"

"Why don't you go get dressed?" Jared nodded toward the upstairs.

"Oh, yeah. Are you going to wait here?"

"I don't think Levi would appreciate if I offered to help."

"Very funny. I just meant, you'll wait at the house?"

"Of course. Where else would I go for ten minutes?" He stuffed his hands in his pockets.

"Ten minutes? Yeah, dream on." I ran back up the last flight of stairs. I stood in front of my closet trying to pick out a dress, but I couldn't. The last thing I wanted to do was dress up and go out. I wanted to sit around and wallow in self-pity.

I settled on a pair of yoga pants and a Tulane sweatshirt. I brushed out my hair but left it down to dry. It wasn't worth the effort of blow-drying it.

"You ready?" Jared turned in his seat at the island when I walked into the kitchen. "Wow, not what I would wear to Brennan's, but to each their own."

"Shut up."

"Okay…you going to tell me what's going on?"

"I'm not going to dinner."

"Any particular reason why?" He tapped a foot on the leg of his stool.

"I can't do this anymore." I slumped down on a stool next to him.

"Do what exactly?" He swiveled to look at me.

"This. Be part of this. I'm not strong enough."

"Are you okay?"

"Do I look okay?"

"No. And since when do you question your strength? You're Miss 'I can do it all.'"

"I can't do it all. I suck." I buried my face in my arms.

"Okay, this isn't funny anymore." He tentatively put a hand on my back. "Do you want me to try to break him out of his meeting?"

I shook my head.

"Are you crying?"

"No." Of course, there were tears streaming down my face.

"What's going on? Wait…are you…Are you pregnant?"

"No!"

"Are you sure? You're acting overly emotional. This can't just be PMS."

"Every time a girl is emotional it's hormones?"

"Not every time…"

"I want to throw something at you."

"Okay…so you are still in there."

"What's wrong with me? I need him. I've never needed anyone before."

"Need him? Like you're so in love with him…"

"Maybe. This is almost physical though. I just need him, and now I know that he doesn't even really love me."

"What? Now you're just talking crazy." He put a hand on the counter next to me. "You can't be comfortable, let's go sit in the living room."

I nodded and followed him. I pulled a pillow onto my lap as I settled onto the couch.

"Okay. Let's start with the most obvious. Levi loves you. Why are you suddenly questioning that?"

"I can't tell you."

"Excuse me?"

"I can't tell you... I can't tell anyone. I think he knows. I think his dad is telling him now. It's going to make him hate me." I started sobbing.

"Damn it, Allie. Don't do this to me." He awkwardly put an arm around me. I leaned into his side. "Levi isn't going to hate you. He couldn't hate you."

"What if he found out his feelings for me weren't his own choice? What if he found out it was all fake?"

"Please just tell me what you're talking about."

"Can I trust you?" I wiped tears off my cheek.

"Of course." His face was serious.

"I mean really trust you."

"Like not to tell Levi something?"

"No. I'm sure he already knows..."

"Then what are you asking?" He searched my face for an answer.

"You're really loyal, right?" I hated even saying the words, but I needed to.

"Okay, now you're seriously freaking me out. I'm fucking loyal to the Laurents, Allie."

"I know. I just had to ask..." I took a deep breath. "Do you know what an enchantress is?"

"Aren't they a spell caster?"

"Yes, but in terms of Pterons."

"There are Pteron spell casters?"

I groaned. "No. Forget the spell casting part. I don't want to explain it all. Suffice it to say there are women who can choose the next Pteron king."

"That's not possible."

"It is."

He shook his head. "It's not."

"Fine. Whatever. I don't know why I even tried."

"Okay, let's just say for a minute that I believe it. What does that have to do with you? Do you think you're one of these women?"

"Yes, Georgina was pretty positive too. I'm kind of like a Pteron heir magnet. They all want me to choose them, take their ring and sleep with them—make them king."

"You already have Levi's ring."

"Something's wrong. Toby still thinks he can get me to choose him…"

"Because he's delusional."

"I don't think he is."

"So what does this have to do with Levi hating you?" Jared actually looked concerned. I wasn't used to seeing that expression on his face.

"You don't get it? He doesn't love me for me, it's all this enchantress stuff." I covered my head with my hands.

"Bullshit. Don't even try to tell me you believe that."

I looked up. "Why not?"

"I thought he told you about the dream."

"You knew?"

"Yes, I knew. The guy was a mess after it. First he was dying to find you then he was dying to forget you. That's when I taught him the art of picking up older girls."

"Ugh. Why older though? Why not girls your age?"

"I'm not that much of an asshole, Allie. Fifteen-year-old girls shouldn't be having sex, let alone having meaningless hook-up sex."

"As compared to fifteen-year-old boys?"

"We weren't boys."

"Fifteen-year-old Pteron boys."

"That doesn't matter anyway. What I'm saying is that he was inconsolable. He pretended to be over it, but I knew he wasn't. And then he met you. I figured it out before he did."

"What? How?"

"At first I thought he just liked the chase, but then I saw the way he got pissed at Owen for even looking at you. He was already possessive like you were his mate."

"You actually think he dreamed the future?"

"I wouldn't have believed it if I hadn't seen him myself."

I closed my eyes. "But that doesn't change that his attraction came from this enchantress thing."

"Come on, don't even try to argue that. Have you looked at yourself in the mirror lately? You're wearing sweats and still look fuckable right now."

"Fuckable?" I laughed.

"Finally a laugh."

"I want him to love me for me." I put a hand over my chest. I was seriously losing it.

"He does."

"I can't lose him."

"You've come a long way in a few months, Princess."

"I know."

"Are you done getting my shirt wet?"

"I think I'm done crying." I didn't make any effort to move. I was too spent, and my head pounded. I let sleep take me.

***

"What the hell are you doing?"

I woke up with a start as I was pushed aside. Levi had Jared by his collar.

"Hey, calm down. It's just me."

"Just you? You think being my friend means you can move in on my mate when I'm not around?" Through my half asleep haze, I saw Levi's eyes turn black.

"Calm down, man. Nothing's going on. I came here like you asked me to."

"I asked you to bring her to dinner. You never showed up."

"We fell asleep." Jared spoke quietly. He was usually pretty good at defusing Levi.

"Get the hell out of my house."

"Calm down."

Levi tightened his grip on Jared's collar. "Get out of this house before I kick the shit out of you."

"Levi!" I grabbed his arm. At first it looked like he was going to shrug me off but he calmed down. "Stay out of this."

"Levi, it's just Jared. He'd never try anything."

Levi's shoulders relaxed, and I kept my eyes glued to him.

Jared gave Levi a funny look. "What was that about?"

"I don't know... I just..."

"Why did you transform so quickly? You are usually the most in control." Jared still looked shaken up.

"He's been doing it more other times too…" Then something hit me. He'd been transforming, I was insanely emotional, having bad headaches, and more attached. What if this was all part of our messed up bond? "It's because we're not bound right."

"What?" Levi turned to me. "We are bound just fine." He picked up my left hand and gently ran a finger over my ring. "You're my mate. Don't ever doubt that." I could feel anger roll off him at the thought of anything else being true.

"Tell him, Allie." Jared sounded more serious than I'd ever heard him.

"Tell me what?"

"Your dad didn't tell you?"

"Tell me what? We were discussing political strategies. He wants to take control over the Hawaiian islands again. Right now, they're independent but… And you really don't care."

I tied my hair up with an elastic I had around my wrist. "Normally I would at least pretend, but this is pretty huge."

"What is it?"

"I don't want you to hate me."

"He's not going to hate you. I already told you that." Jared shook his head. "Do you want me to stay or go?"

"Stay. That way if Levi decides he wants nothing to do with me, you can at least drive me back to my dorm." Would he be disgusted that the feelings he felt for me weren't even his own? Would he blame me?

Levi put a hand on both of my shoulders and looked me right in the eye. "What's going on? There's nothing in the world that could do that."

I sat back down on the couch. Levi sat down right next to me. "I don't know where to start."

"Let me do this." Jared crossed his arms. "Both Allie and your grandma think she's an enchantress—which does not mean she's a spell caster. She supposedly has the power to pick the next king, and every Pteron heir who gets near her wants to jump her."

Levi put an arm around me protectively as soon as Jared said the last part.

Jared groaned. "I'm not an heir, idiot."

"My grandmother believes this?" Levi ran a hand through his hair. He only did that when he was upset or nervous.

I struggled to swallow. "Yeah...nothing else makes sense."

"But what does this have to do with our bond? You're obviously with me, so I'm going to be king anyway." His eyes locked with mine, like he was searching for words I wasn't saying.

"It should have broken the attraction of the others...it should be over. Your grandmother and Toby seem to think I can still choose someone else unless we fix this."

"But I gave you my ring. We consummated it."

"You didn't give me a choice. When I accepted the ring, I didn't know what I was accepting. But the real issue is whether any of your feelings for me are really yours."

"Of course my feelings are my own, and the bond is there, we'll figure out how to fix any issues with it." He was taking the news way better than I expected. I kept waiting for the floor to drop out from under me.

A look of understanding crossed his face. "Is that why you look so upset? Why you didn't show up at dinner?"

"Mostly. I also just felt lousy." Was he really more worried about me than the bomb I'd just dropped on him?

"She was missing you…and on that note, I'm out of here. Judging by the death grip he has on you, I don't think you have to worry about Levi kicking you out tonight."

"Good night, Jared." I didn't bother to turn around. I knew he was already halfway out the door.

"What do we do now?" Levi asked softly.

We needed to talk things out, but I was afraid of making things worse. I was just so relieved he hadn't walked away from me. "I don't know. Right now I just want to curl up in bed with you."

"Your wish is my command." He picked me up and carried me upstairs.

I was snuggling into his side when he whispered in my ear. "I'm glad you don't need extra adrenaline when we're together."

"What?" I sat up.

He grinned. "I never imagined you'd like to have sex when you think you'll get caught."

"What? Did Hailey tell you?"

"Of course not. We have all of Toby's calls and messages recorded. I was a little surprised at first, but anyone who actually knew you would have figured out it wasn't you. 'How could I ever be over you or your body?' That's not Allie talk. It was Anne, wasn't it?"

"Yes." I buried my face in his shoulder.

"I liked your response to not being able to walk after a night with him. Is that supposed to be a good thing? Now that's more like you."

"You're mighty calm about this."

"It's easy to be when you're in bed with me. I have to admit, it's a good thing you told me that Toby kissed you. The hot tub comment may have sent me on a war path otherwise."

"Yeah... I think Hailey was in shock."

"You didn't tell her?"

"I felt too icky. I told you because I needed it all out in the open."

"Are you more awake now?"

"Why?" I picked my head up.

"You bailed on me for dinner, but I did bring you back something."

"What?"

"Hold on." He dashed out of bed and I heard him taking the stairs two at a time. He reappeared a minute later. I knew what would be in his hand before he stepped through the doorway.

"Whipped cream?"

"I'd take you and whipped cream over Bananas Foster any day." He referred to the Brennan's dessert specialty I loved.

"You're forgetting something very important."

"And what's that?" He pulled back the blankets.

"I'm the one who's going to be enjoying the whipped cream."

Chapter Fourteen

"What exactly is a Maid supposed to do?" Anne asked as we sat squashed in the back of Michelle's Camry on the way to a fitting. Michelle was the only one of us allowed to keep a car on campus, since the rest of us were freshman.

"We're supposed to smile and look pretty, and to make sure Allie doesn't ruin her dress when she uses the bathroom." Michelle looked at us in the rearview mirror.

Anne nodded. "Got it. We're like bridesmaids."

"Except the ball isn't my wedding." I fidgeted. Being stuck in the middle seat is never fun.

"Nope, that's not until this summer." Hailey turned back to look at us. I could tell she'd been grinning when she made the wedding comment. "I can't wait to see my dress." Hailey may have been talking about the outfit, but it was the position she was most excited about.

"Are our dresses going to be like Hailey's?" Tiffany asked. "Or are they just a little different?"

"Probably similar, but they won't be quite as fancy." Michelle turned onto the Laurents' street. My stomach churned the way it always did when I thought about seeing Robert.

Tiffany put a hand on my shoulder. "Maybe he won't be home. He isn't exactly going to be part of the fitting."

"You're right. I don't know why I let him intimidate me so much."

She smiled. "He's a supernatural king and your future father-in-law. I think I know why."

"Maybe it isn't so crazy…"

Michelle pulled into the drive, and even she looked nervous as she stepped out. I'd insisted Hailey sit in front in hopes that the two would talk, but I don't think it did any good. They both jumped to walk in at my side. I held back a smile. Like there was any competition. Everyone knew whose side I'd take every time. Still, I was glad Michelle was going to be a maid. I knew it was an important olive branch to extend.

Helen opened the door with a huge grin on her face. "Come in, come in." She gave me a hug and a kiss on the cheek before greeting the rest of the girls. We followed her back into her sewing room.

"Is that Allie's dress?" Anne's mouth fell open when she caught sight of my gown. "Oh my gosh, it's amazing."

"I'm so glad you think so." Helen beamed. "Should we do Allie first, or do you girls want to see your dresses?"

"Allie first. I can't wait." Hailey grinned. My expression matched hers. I hadn't had time to think about it much over the past few weeks, but I was definitely excited to try it on again. I still couldn't believe how little time had passed. Jess hadn't even missed her first day of class yet because NYU was still on break. Suddenly, I lost all interest in trying it on. I wasn't supposed to be enjoying things. My head throbbed and I felt dizzy.

"Allie? Are you okay?" Helen asked with concern.

"Yeah, I was just thinking about something."

"Why don't you take a seat, sweetie. We'll let the girls go first." She put a hand on my shoulder.

I smiled, glad she let it go so easily. I took a seat on an upholstered chair and watched my friends try on their black dresses. The Maid dresses were similar to Hailey's but they didn't have the ruby embellishment. Each dress was cut a little differently. Anne's was strapless, Tiffany's was a halter, and Michelle's had spaghetti straps. It was hard to stay in a bad mood watching everyone dressing up. I had a smile on my face when I tried on my gown again. This time I had my silver heels with me. The room went speechless when Helen zipped me up.

"Wow. Levi is going to die." Anne actually jumped up and down.

"He is, isn't he?" Helen smiled. I wondered if it was awkward for her to talk about her son like that.

"Is there anything else we need to do or bring that night?" Tiffany asked.

"Just yourselves. I have escorts set up for everyone."

"Escorts?" Tiffany asked nervously.

"You didn't have to go through all of that trouble Mrs. Laurent." Hailey smiled politely, but I could tell she was nervous about who she'd be paired up with.

"Tiffany, you'll be with Jared. Anne, you're with Owen."

"Owen? Nice." Anne grinned. Hailey shook her head. "What? I'm not gonna lie. Your brother's hot."

Tiffany hadn't said a word, but she paled. We all knew she had a crush on Jared, but I wasn't sure how she'd feel about having him as a date for the evening.

"Who am I paired up with?" Michelle asked impatiently. I could tell she was struggling to be polite.

Helen smiled. "As is expected, you will both be paired with humans."

"What humans?" Hailey asked.

"Kyle and Kent Applewood."

"Mark Applewood's sons?" Michelle asked, her mouth hanging open.

"Yes, their father is Mark Applewood." Helen smiled. She had expected the reaction.

"And I thought going with a prince was pretty cool." I laughed. The Applewoods owned several major sport franchises in the southeast. They were some of the most eligible bachelors of our generation.

"Your date's been waiting to escort you for a long time." Helen smiled before putting a few pins in my dress.

"There's no one else I'd rather go with." I meant it with all my heart.

***

The next few weeks flew by, and I still hadn't heard anything about Jess. I pretended to concentrate on my school work, but it was impossible. The only reason I was looking forward to the ball was that it was another opportunity to meet others in The Society.

"There's one more thing." Hailey held out a wooden box with a crow engraved on the top. We were all getting ready in my suite at the hotel. The ball was being held downstairs.

"Is this…"

"Yeah."

I opened the box and gasped as I touched the glittering ruby tiara. "This can't be for real."

"Wow, that's gorgeous." Anne came up behind me. "Put it on."

I was awe struck. It was a real tiara, the kind that only a princess would wear. "I can't. My hands are shaking."

"I'll do it." Hailey picked it up and placed it on my head. I was wearing my hair mostly down with just a little pulled back. Levi always loved when I wore it that way.

"How does it look?" I asked because everyone was staring at me.

"Incredible. You look incredible." Michelle smiled.

I walked into the bathroom so I could look at myself in the full-length mirror. "I can't believe I actually get to wear all of this."

"You look gorgeous." Tiffany put a hand on my arm.

"So do you. All of you look amazing." They did. I hoped their dates were prepared.

"Are we ready, then?" Hailey asked.

I let out a slow, deep breath. "Yes. Are the guys waiting?"

"I think they're in the lobby. We can head down, but why don't you wait here for Levi," Michelle suggested.

"That's probably a good idea." I was nervous, and Levi had a way of calming me down.

"See you in a few." Hailey squeezed my hand before walking out of the room.

A knock on the door let me know Levi was there already. I opened it, stepping back to let him in.

"You—you look—" He appeared awe struck too.

"Are you actually speechless?"

He nodded. "Almost. You look amazing." He reached out for my hands. "Absolutely amazing."

"You look great, too." He did. I loved how his tux fit him perfectly. It was charcoal gray with a vest—a different look for him, and it worked just like all the others.

"Not like you." He let go of one of my hands so he could twirl me around. "I really don't want to leave this room, but I'll admit I do want to show you off."

"I hope I don't embarrass myself."

"Why would you? You look incredible. All you have to do is smile and be yourself."

"Everyone's going to be sizing me up, trying to see if you picked the right mate." It was easy to forget that as far as anyone else knew, Levi had just randomly found a mate.

"Oh, I picked the right mate." He leaned over and kissed me lightly. "I want to do a whole lot more than that, but I'll probably be killed if I mess up your hair and makeup."

"Probably. We should go anyway. Everyone's waiting."

"Ready, my love?" He held out his arm.

I linked my arm with his. "Ready."

We kissed again in the elevator, and his lips promised that there would be a lot more to follow later.

When we reached the lobby, we walked directly to the ballroom. Levi's parents waited in the foyer, right in front of the large entrance doors. I could hear music from within the room, and I wondered what the guests were doing. Would they all be waiting for us to come in?

"Breathtaking." Helen embraced me warmly.

"You look amazing, and thanks so much for this gorgeous dress."

"She enjoyed making it, Allie, and you do look stunning." Robert gave me that unnerving smile of his.

"Thank you."

"Are they ready for us?" Levi nodded to the closed doors of the ballroom.

Robert waved his arm. "Make your entrance."

"Show time." Levi squeezed my hand.

He knocked on the door twice and both doors swung open for us. I let him lead me through the dark entryway. We took a few steps in and my breath hitched. The room was absolutely incredible. I'd been in plenty of ballrooms, but none had ever looked like this one did that night. Strings of crystal and ruby lights hung down from the ceilings, while the dance floor was lined with red roses, each with tiny crystals tied onto the stems. But it wasn't the décor that made me lose my breath, it was the people. The room was full of elegantly dressed men and woman who were all watching us. If it weren't for Levi's strong hand on my back, I might have had a serious problem continuing into the room. I'm usually not intimidated by large crowds, but knowing that the most important and influential members of The Society and the world were in that room was a lot to handle.

Levi led me over to the side just as his father and mother walked in. Helen didn't look even remotely nervous as she made her elegant entrance. I wondered if I'd ever be as comfortable with it.

Robert and Helen stopped in the middle of the dance floor. Robert nodded to Levi, and we joined them.

Robert cleared his throat and waited for the voices to quiet. "Welcome. We are thrilled to have each of you here tonight. This has been an exciting year for our family and The Society. Most importantly, Leviathan has selected his mate, and your future queen. I have had the pleasure of getting to know her well over the past few months, and I assure you, she will be excellent for the position."

Gotten to know me well? I don't think I would have put it quite that way.

"Although traditionally my queen and I would have the first dance, we have decided to hand that honor over to Leviathan and Allison tonight."

I took a deep breath as a waltz began to play. Levi led me perfectly, and I was able to forget everything else around me. The last time he'd danced with me in such a formal setting, he told me he loved me. I told him I didn't feel the same way. I couldn't believe it had been less than six months since that night.

The crowd broke into applause as the song ended. I leaned up and whispered in his ear. "I love you."

"I love you too, Al. I love you, too." He took my hand and led me over to the side so his parents could take their turn.

"Wow, you guys are the most adorable couple ever." Anne dragged Owen with her as she came to join us.

"We are, aren't we?" Levi put an arm around my shoulder.

"You make it sound like you've never seen them together." Owen seemed to like arguing with Anne. She brought out a weird side in him.

She turned to him with a hand on her hip. "They just look so different tonight—so royal."

"Because they are royal. He's the prince and she's his princess."

Anne tapped Tiffany on the shoulder. "Tiff, can we change dates? Mine's defective."

Levi and I both laughed.

Jared answered for the speechless Tiffany. By the smile on her face earlier, she had no interest in changing dates. "I'd be happy to be both of your dates." Jared raised an eyebrow.

"No, that won't be necessary." Owen took Anne's arm. "Let's give Allie and Levi some space."

Jared and Tiffany followed them.

"Wow…drama." Levi laughed.

"I know…normally I'd say it's a lovers' spat, but I really don't think they've slept together."

"Who's slept together?" Hailey came up behind us, without her date.

"Your brother and Anne." Levi grinned.

"Ewww, please tell me they haven't."

"They haven't. Ignore him." I rolled my eyes. "Where's your date, Hail?"

"My escort was boring me to death talking about football."

I laughed. "It's kind of early in the night to get bored."

"Maybe he wants me to do what Michelle's doing with his brother."

I followed her gaze to where Michelle was hanging all over her date. "The Applewoods are cute."

"Excuse me?" Levi put an arm around my waist.

"I said cute. You're hot and sexy, big difference."

"Hot and sexy?" He pulled me against his side. "And you haven't even had anything to drink yet."

I bit my lip flirtatiously. "You could change that." Levi and I always teased each other, and I loved it. Toby and I were so much more formal about things. I could really be myself with Levi, and I was pretty sure he could say the same thing.

"I will." He kissed my forehead before leaving Hailey and I to talk. I had to give Levi credit, he always knew when that's what I wanted.

"You two made quite the entrance." Hailey fidgeted with her bracelet.

"Yeah? Did I look okay?"

"Fantastic. All the guys who hadn't seen you yet are now joking about how Levi's never going to get anything done."

"What? Oh. Because we'll be in bed a lot?"

"Lovely conversation topic, huh?"

"Well, if someone says it in front of you again, just say it's a good thing Pterons don't need a lot of sleep."

Hailey laughed. "I'm glad you're in a good mood. I've been worried."

"Yeah, I know I've been a grump. I'm just—"

"Scared for Jess? I understand. I swear we're going to get her."

"I know."

"Miss me?" Levi handed me a drink. I didn't need to taste it to know what kind it was.

"A little."

His arms came around me, and he pulled me back into his chest. "It's kind of painful to be apart tonight. You look so good."

"Don't I look just as good from a distance?"

"Yes, but then I can't touch you."

"And on that note, I'm going to find my date." Hailey nodded toward where he stood watching us. "I might need a drink first though."

I laughed. "I'm sure you can find something to talk about."

"We'll see." Hailey gave me a half wave before disappearing into the crowd.

"Ready to make the rounds?" Levi ran a hand down my bare arm. It gave me goose bumps.

"Sure. Ready as I'll ever be." I took a quick sip of the signature drink Levi still hadn't told me the name of.

"All right, my princess, let's meet the rest of your subjects."

"Do you have to use terms like that?"

"What? It's the truth." He slipped his arm over my shoulder.

"It just makes things weirder."

"Did you forget what's on your head, love?" He touched my tiara.

"No." How could I forget? The thing weighed a lot. That's something people don't tell you, a real tiara is heavy.

"You're a princess. One day soon you'll be a queen. These people are your subjects." He kissed me gently on the lips before moving his arm to my waist, leading me toward the crowds.

We hadn't made it far when Robert grabbed Levi's arm. "We have some unexpected guests."

I turned to follow Robert's gaze and saw a middle-aged man with a shock of gray hair and a younger man that was probably in his early twenties.

"The Dalys are here?" Levi's voice was strained. He tightened his hold on my waist. "They never come."

"Evidently, they decided it was worth it this time." Robert gave Levi a look. "We couldn't refuse them entrance."

"She knows." Levi didn't look at me when he said it.

"I know what?"

He looked away. "What you are."

I startled, and tried to move out of his arm. "What? You knew this whole time? You acted surprised!"

Anger boiled inside me. He was still lying to me.

"I never said I didn't know...and I still didn't understand how it affected us."

"That's great, absolutely great." I tried to pull away from Levi again.

"What are you doing?"

"Getting away from you."

"No," he hissed. "You can't."

While we were arguing, the Dalys had moved closer. That's when it hit me. I remembered the name from when I was with the cougars. This was another heir.

"Hello, Robert. Leviathan." The older man spoke first. "And Allison, how lovely to finally meet you."

The older man spoke, but it was the younger one who reached out a hand to mine. "You truly are the most beautiful woman I've ever seen."

I gave him my hand, strangely attracted to this guy I'd just met. It wasn't like it was with Levi, but there was no question there was something there. "Thank you. I don't think I caught your name."

"Cade. It's a pleasure to meet you."

I felt a tug and suddenly my hand wasn't in Cade's anymore. "If you'll excuse me, my mate and I have many others to greet tonight."

Cade turned to Levi. "I'd like to request a dance with Allison."

"Request denied. She won't be dancing with anyone but me." He pushed me partially behind him.

"But it's customary. I am allowed one dance." Cade took a step toward me.

"And I'm overruling that." Levi turned, pulling me with him.

Cade raised his voice. "No. I demand my dance. You can't break the rules."

Levi turned around and scowled at Cade. "I just did."

"Levi." Robert's voice was scratchy. "He has the right to one dance."

Was this really over whether Cade could dance with me? Did an heir always have the right to dance with the prince's mate?

Levi let out a low growl. Listening to the guttural noise reminded me that he wasn't human. "Fine. One dance, but you better not upset her."

"Don't I get a say in who I dance with?" I knew I should probably keep my mouth shut, but I refused to just sit back and listen to them talking about me.

"No." Levi and Cade said at once.

I searched the room for help. The tension was suffocating, and at that moment I was angry with Levi, and a mix of attracted and scared of Cade.

"Surely you wouldn't mind giving my son one dance?" the so far pleasant senior Daly asked.

Considering he bothered to ask me, I wasn't going to deny the request. "I suppose I could."

Cade's smile was only matched by Levi's scowl.

Cade held out a hand, and I accepted it. I figured one dance couldn't be that bad. He led me across the dance floor.

The music was slow, so slow that it was almost hard to dance to. Cade put one hand on my shoulder and the other clasped my hand. "It's true. I didn't believe it until I saw you."

"What's true?" I had a good idea what he was referring to, but playing stupid was sometimes the best option in those sorts of situations.

"That you have the power to choose. When I heard Levi found a mate, I figured it was only a matter of time before you gave him his heir. It wasn't until my father heard that you had also dated the Blackwell heir that we knew what you were. He'd sensed the possibility over a year ago but thought he was out of his mind."

"How did he hear? Is my dating life that public?"

He smiled. "A potential mate of a prince must realize her life is no longer hers to keep private."

"It's still my life."

"I know, sweetheart."

"Sweetheart? Do you really think it's appropriate to call me that?"

He leaned in closer. "You will be my mate soon enough...why not start now?"

"Your mate?" That's when I thought over his prior potential mate comment. "Do you really think I won't remain Levi's mate?"

"I know you feel it." He leaned in to whisper. "It's too incredible not to."

"Feel what?"

"Do you always play dumb? You seem otherwise intelligent."

"Where are you from?"

He moved in closer to me. "L.A."

"You're from L.A.?"

"Does that surprise you?" He moved his hand slightly lower on my back.

"You don't talk like someone from L.A." I couldn't place his accent, it sounded vaguely Italian, but I wasn't the best judge.

He laughed. "That's because I spent most of my life in Europe. I only moved back last year after I graduated."

"How old are you?"

"Twenty-three. Why, are you worried about an age difference?"

"No," I answered quickly. "I was just wondering."

He put a hand under my chin. "I like you, Allison. We're going to have a great time together."

I turned my head, forcing him to let go of my chin. "It's Allie." I didn't even let Levi call me by my full name. "Don't sound so confident. I already made my choice.

"No you haven't, and Allie? I like the nickname."

The song ended, and I sighed with relief.

He ran a finger down my arm. "I'm staying at the hotel for the next few days. I wouldn't mind a visit."

"I don't—"

"Dance is over." Levi grabbed my arm, partially blocking Cade from view.

"That was lovely, Allie. I look forward to spending more time with you soon."

I nodded, not sure what to do.

"What were you talking about?" Levi handed me a glass of wine.

"What do you think?"

"You're not actually angry with me, are you?"

I groaned. "I don't know what to feel." I still couldn't believe he hadn't told me he'd known about the enchantress stuff.

"I didn't know much, I just knew you were something more than a regular human. I would have told you, but my dad told me it could mess things up worse."

I wrapped my arms around myself. "Your dad doesn't always have the answers."

"I know…and I'm sorry. I want to fix this as much as you do."

"So we can be together or so you can be king?"

"You can't doubt my feelings for you." He took my hand, forcing my arms down.

"I don't know what I believe anymore." I tried to pull my hand from his.

He held my hand tighter. "Please, don't let this get to you. It's nothing."

"Keep telling yourself that." I didn't get a chance to walk off.

"Allie." Toby said my name like he was savoring it.

Levi released my hand only to put an arm around me again. I didn't mind once I realized who Toby was with. "Leviathan, how nice to see you again." The old man next to Toby talked to Levi, but his eyes never left me.

"What brings you here tonight?" Robert, materializing out of nowhere, didn't even let Levi respond for himself.

"That's an unnecessary question, Robert." The old man still watched me like a hawk.

"Who's the boy?" Robert stepped in front of me. It was the first time he'd done anything protective.

"I forget. You've never met my grandson, have you?"

"It's funny how it's the first time you've publicly acknowledged him."

"We had our reasons for keeping his presence quiet, but I don't believe for a second you're surprised. You're aware of my grandson's relationship with Allison Davis, aren't you?"

"His prior relationship." Robert hadn't moved from his position in front of me.

"He had her first. He never acquiesced to her leaving. She's his."

Robert grunted. "He never took her as a mate. She was free to go where she pleased."

"You expect us to believe she came to New Orleans by chance? The girl's a New Yorker. She was enrolled at Princeton with my grandson. If you hadn't meddled, she'd be there now."

Normally I would have complained about someone speaking like I wasn't there, but I was terrified of this guy. If Robert was scary, this guy was petrifying. It was like he emitted waves of fear.

Robert didn't miss a beat. "Her reasons for coming to New Orleans have nothing to do with the matter." Georgina was right—Robert had to have had something to do with my dad buying the hotel.

The old man sneered. "Allie never accepted your son. If she had, it would be over."

Robert laughed dryly. "Are you really going to pretend to believe the old enchantress stories?"

"You know as well as I do that it's true. She chose to lay with Toby first, she's a Blackwell, and the crown will move."

"Lay with?" I couldn't stay quiet any longer. For some reason, I got adrenaline rushes that allowed me to stand up to scary men. "Did I sleep with Toby? Yes, but I had no idea he wasn't just my human boyfriend. At least Levi told me what he was."

I didn't need to turn around to know that Levi was probably smiling.

"I formally request my dance." Toby spoke for the first time since saying my name.

"First Cade, and now you? This is ridiculous. I'm not just some toy that can be passed around."

"Cade? The Dalys are here?" The elder Blackwell glanced around.

Robert nodded. "Unfortunately."

"What do they hope to accomplish? Surely they can't believe the girl would pick a boy she doesn't even know."

"None of this should even be happening. Levi is the rightful heir to the throne. I'm sure they'll have an heir soon, ending all of this." Robert clasped his hands together like he was trying to stop himself from hurting Mr. Blackwell.

Mr. Blackwell's eyes darkened. "How would that end anything? If their bond isn't final, then the child wouldn't be a true heir."

I could feel the tension ratcheting. If someone didn't do something, there would be a fight. "Stop! Stop talking about who I will or will not be having children with. This is all too much." I turned to walk away when I felt a tight grip on my arm.

"You owe my grandson a dance." The elder Blackwell seethed with anger. I wanted to argue, but all I could do was nod.

Levi pulled me into his arms, running his hand over my now tender skin. "You touch her again, and I will kill you."

"Don't threaten me, child."

"If he doesn't do it, I will. You have no right to lay a hand on her." Robert once again blocked me.

"Tell her to give Toby the dance, and I won't have to. You know he is owed it."

Robert turned, not bothering to cover the annoyance and anger on his face. Even though I knew it wasn't directed at me, it still got me. "Dance with the boy."

I nodded, still not sure how to respond.

Toby gently took my hand. "I'm sorry," he whispered in my ear as we moved onto the dance floor.

"He's horrible."

"I'll protect you from him. Besides, he won't be angry once you come back."

"I'm not coming back."

"You have to. If not for me, do it for Jess." His eyes were filled with emotion. He seemed almost as overwhelmed as me.

"Jess? I thought she was okay…"

"I'm not in charge anymore…my grandfather took over."

"What?" My head started to spin.

Toby caught me before I could fall. Still lightheaded, I didn't complain about the contact. "He's going to hold off another two weeks, but that's all I can get. He wants this situation taken care of."

"Allie, are you okay?" Levi came up beside me.

"Our dance isn't over," Toby snapped.

"She almost fell."

"I caught her."

Levi reluctantly walked away. This dance thing must have been really official for him to be giving up so easily.

"You have two weeks, Allie. Two weeks or he's going to do it."

"Do what?"

Toby lowered his voice. "Get rid of her."

FOUND

"How can you let that happen? Jess is your friend too!"

"I had no choice, and there's an easy solution. Just pick me."

"There has to be another way..." I needed there to be.

"There isn't." He leaned over and kissed me on the cheek. I moved away.

"Is being with him really worth an innocent girl's life?" With that he walked away.

I was left speechless in the middle of the dance floor.

"Are you okay?" Levi's comforting arms wrapped around me.

I shook my head, unable to speak.

"What did he do to you?"

I could feel the tears starting. "Can you get us out of here?"

"Yes, of course."

I barely realized what was happening as Levi led us out of the room. I felt too sick to think. I leaned into the arm Levi offered as we waited for the elevator to take us to the basement.

"No one will bother us here." He closed the door to our safe room before I could argue.

"We can't stay in here all night."

"Since we're not in lockdown, we can open the door at any time."

"I can't do this, Levi."

"Do what?" He led me over to the couch. That piece of furniture had been conveniently missing the last time I'd been there.

"Let Jess spend another minute with those horrible people. Toby said his grandfather was going to kill her if I didn't come."

"And you think he won't kill her if you turn yourself over?" His voice wasn't cold, but nothing could make his words easier to accept.

"It doesn't matter. I can't just sit here. I have to do something."

He put a hand on my bare shoulder. "There's nothing you can do. You need to let me take care of this."

I wanted to argue, but it wasn't going to help anything. I was going to have to figure things out on my own. I needed time to think, and I needed some space. I wasn't going to get any space in our safe room. "We can go back to the party."

"We don't have to."

"I want to. It's our night, we should be there."

"If you're sure." He reluctantly stood up. "We're still going back to the house tonight, right?"

I let out a deep breath. "Yes." I was angry at Levi for not telling me he knew about the enchantress thing, but the truth was, I was doing the same thing—keeping secrets.

"All right."

We took the elevator upstairs and walked back into the ballroom.

"There you are." Hailey grabbed my arm. "Where have you guys been? Things are getting crazy."

"Crazy?" Levi asked.

Hailey looked worried. "Your admirers were about to tear this place apart looking for you."

Levi groaned. "Why? They've each had their dance. They don't get anything else."

Hailey played with her bracelet again. "It's insane, even your dad looks worried, Levi."

"I need to find him, but I'm not leaving Allie. Where are Jared and Owen?"

"The last I saw, Anne and Tiffany actually had them dancing."

"Seriously? If everything else wasn't so crazy, I'd love to see that."

I jumped in. "Should I just go? Would that make it easier?"

Levi seemed to think about it for a minute. "No. We need to just face them head on again. If you run, it looks like you have a reason to."

"It's not like I'm in trouble…"

"No, but they want it to look like we're in trouble."

"This is so dumb."

"I agree, hopefully we can end all this soon."

"Allison, may I have a word with you?" The elder Blackwell stopped several feet from us, yet I still shivered.

Levi moved in front of me. "Anything you have to say to her can be said in front of me."

"Fine. I was just going to comment on how beautiful those green eyes of yours are. I wonder where I've seen ones like them before." He ran a hand through his beard. "Oh wait, I remember. Your mother."

"My mother? How do you know my mother?"

He grinned. "Lovely meeting you, Allison." He started walking away.

"Wait! How do you know my mother?"

Levi put a hand on my arm. "He's just trying to bait you."

"It worked. I need to get my phone. It's in my room upstairs."

"No, it's not." He pulled my phone out of his jacket pocket.

"How'd you get that?"

"I grabbed it on the way out of your room. I know how much you hate to be separated from it. Call her."

I hit the speed dial for my mom.

"Allie?" Mom picked up right away.

"Hi, Mom. Are you all right?"

"Of course, I'm all right. Why would you ask? It's kind of loud, where are you?"

"At a party. I just wanted to tell you I love you."

"Are you okay, sweetie?"

"Fine."

"Well, I love you too."

"I'll call you tomorrow." I hung up and let out a sigh of relief.

"See, he's just baiting you."

I nodded, but it could still have been a threat. There was no way I was just sitting back anymore.

Chapter Fifteen

Slipping past Pterons isn't easy, but it is possible. I woke up on the Monday after the ball on a mission. It was time to get Jess back.

I slept in as late as possible, well aware that talking to Hailey more than I had to was a bad idea. She'd become incredibly good at reading my mood, and she'd know I was up to something if I gave her a chance to find out. I finished my breakfast twice as fast as normal and rushed to class. I was already seated in Organic Chem when Jared sat down next to me.

"Morning, Princess."

"Good morning," I mumbled, studying my pen.

"What? No snazzy retort?"

"Snazzy retort?"

He grinned. "I thought it sounded fun."

I set aside my pen. I'd tip him off if I didn't respond to his ribbing. "I love how you only let your geek side out around me."

"I don't have a geek side." The defensive tone in his voice was comical.

"Yes, you do."

He set up his laptop. "It takes one to know one."

"I don't deny mine. I own up."

"Yeah, I know." He laughed. "Hey, where's the computer? Did you break it already?"

"Very funny. I forgot to charge it."

"Add a ditsy side to the geeky one."

"I won't own up to that one. Forgetting to charge a computer doesn't make me ditzy." That was my cover story—I couldn't bring my computer where I was going.

At least I could keep things light with Jared. I was actually kind of enjoying the banter. Unfortunately, he was going to hate me for what I was about to do.

The professor started class, and I dutifully took notes even though I knew I'd be leaving my notebook behind.

I waited twenty minutes for good measure before tapping Jared on the shoulder. "Bathroom," I mouthed while gesturing to the door.

He nodded before turning back to his computer. He'd tried to follow me to the bathroom once during class and regretted it quickly. I'd been counting on him remembering that lesson. The solution to the bathroom problem was to plant a Pteron in the hallway outside my classes. The one on Mondays was a guy, so I knew he couldn't follow me in either.

Pushing open the wood door, I glanced over my shoulder and smiled at the Pteron. He half smiled in greeting as I let the door close behind me.

Without wasting any time, I climbed on the vanity and reached up to open the window. It didn't budge at first, but I refused to panic. I took a deep breath and tried again. It squeaked as it opened, and I tensed waiting for the guard to run in. He didn't.

The window wasn't huge, but I was pretty sure I could squeeze through it. I hoped no one was outside at that moment, because I would have flashed anyone passing by. Wearing a skirt wasn't ideal, but jeans would have been too casual for what I was doing. I put my head through first, wiggling the rest of myself through while trying to hold on so I wouldn't fall. Thankfully it was a first floor bathroom, but that didn't mean falling into the bushes would feel good. I made it out in one piece and stopped to smooth out my skirt.

I checked my watch before taking a quick walk over to the front of campus, relieved to see the white cab waiting along the curb. "The Crescent City Hotel, please."

I tried to relax, but it was impossible. I watched the houses as we drove down St. Charles Avenue. I was getting ready to do something that was either incredibly brave or incredibly stupid. Most likely it was a little of both. Either way, it wasn't something I wanted to do.

I paid the driver and walked into the lobby.

"Allie?" Billy's upbeat voice called out to me before I reached the elevators.

"Hey, Billy." I took off my sunglasses and faced him.

"What are you doing here? I haven't seen you in ages." Billy was such a nice guy. He was also a bellboy at my dad's hotel who had a huge crush on Jess. The manager of the hotel, a Pteron, had let all of the non-Society staff off for the night of the ball, so it had been a long time since we'd run into each other.

"I'm just meeting someone."

"Okay, cool." He looked nervous, and I knew what he was about to ask. "Have you heard from Jess?"

"Not for a few weeks." That part was true.

"Oh, that's cool."

"Yeah. Well, it was nice seeing you." I smiled.

"Same to you. I should get back to work."

"See ya around."

I entered the elevator without running into anyone else and hit the button for the fifth floor. I took a deep breath and let it out slowly. I could do this. The trick was to stay calm. The elevator reached the fifth floor, and I got off. I stalled outside the room for a moment before I got up the nerve to knock.

"Hi, come on in." His voice was breathy, and his eyes matched. I steadied myself as I walked into Cade's suite. I could handle this. I'd put so much work into getting down to the hotel by myself, I couldn't screw this up.

I stepped inside and waited as he closed and locked the door behind me. Why'd he have to lock it? I looked around the room and my heart sunk. He had the curtains drawn and candles lit. Never mind that it was the middle of the afternoon.

"Going all out, huh?" I gestured to the white pillar candles. Other than the ambiance, the suite looked a whole lot like the one I had a few floors above.

"We're only going to get one first time together." His eyes smoldered.

"Oh—um, we're not actually… I didn't come here to sleep with you." I could barely speak coherently. The nerves and the message his eyes and body were sending me did not make a good combination.

"Are you sure about that?"

I forced myself to look away from his eyes, and I took all of him in. The top few buttons of his shirt were unbuttoned, giving me a pretty good view of his chest.

Pterons all seemed to have incredible physiques, and Cade's chiseled body was no exception. It was all way too much. "Would you mind turning on some lights?"

"Are you nervous?" He smiled, but it wasn't in a condescending way. He seemed to actually care.

"Very." Just not for the reason he thought.

"Here, I'll pour us some wine. It'll help you relax."

"Wine?"

"A Barbera from our family's estate. I assure you, it's good," he explained proudly. Evidently the Laurents weren't the only ones with wine interests.

"Would it be okay if I sat down?"

"Of course. Take a seat."

I sat on the edge of the couch as I waited for Cade to pour the wine and join me.

He handed me a glass before raising his own. "To a beautiful woman and my future mate."

I smiled and put the glass to my lips, but I didn't sip. There was no way I was drinking in that situation.

"I'm so glad you decided to stop by. I was beginning to think you weren't going to." He sat down next to me, leaving less than a socially acceptable amount of space between us. If either of us moved our legs, they would have been touching.

"It's hard for me to get out by myself." I was already waiting for my cell phone to vibrate in my purse again. It had been doing it every few minutes since I'd slipped into the cab.

"I understand Levi's reluctance to let you out unprotected. I'll do the same. You can never be too safe."

"You keep talking like our being together is inevitable." I swirled around the wine in my glass.

"Isn't it?" He leaned forward and put a hand on my leg. I shifted, hoping he'd get the hint and move it. He didn't. Instead he slowly moved it further up. I really shouldn't have worn a skirt. I stood up.

He laughed lightly. "I'm not going to bite."

"I didn't come here for that."

"Then what are you here for?" He looked at me curiously.

"I have a proposition for you."

"A proposition?" He arched an eyebrow. "The only proposition I'm interested in involves you and me in that bed, with my ring on your finger." He nodded toward the closed door to his bedroom.

I shook my head, willing away the image he'd planted. "Not happening today."

"Today? Does that mean it might happen later…" He sat up more.

"Will you hear me out?"

"Yes, sit back down. I promise I'll keep my hands to myself."

I sat down. "You want to be king." I wasn't asking a question. I already knew the answer.

He smiled. "Yes."

"The only way that is going to happen is through me, right?"

He nodded. "Uh huh."

"If you help me, I'll make sure you're a king."

"What do you need help with? Although, I'd do nearly anything to get you as my mate…"

"The Blackwells have my friend. I think they're going to kill her if I don't pick Toby."

"And Levi isn't retrieving her?" Cade didn't try to hide his surprise.

"He says he needs to wait, but I can't wait any longer. She's innocent—she doesn't deserve this." Meeting Toby's grandfather had been the proverbial nail in the coffin. I was done waiting around.

"Let me get this straight. If I get your friend for you, you'll make me king? What proof do I have that you'll keep your word?" He looked torn. Like he wanted to trust me but couldn't.

"I'll swear it in any way I have to." I made myself look at him as I said it. He needed to know I was serious.

"You'll do a formal oath swearing that you will choose me to be your mate?"

I shook my head. "No."

He sipped his wine. "You just said…"

"I just said I'd make you a king."

"That's the same thing."

"It's not. Just trust me on this."

"I'll need the usual witnesses, and of course some consideration."

"Consideration?" I set aside my wine. I had no idea what a sworn oath was, but I figured it was the only way he was going to agree.

"To make it binding…just like a contract."

"You want money?"

He smiled. "I'd take a kiss instead."

"How about my bracelet? It's worth at least a few hundred." I started to unlatch it.

He put a hand on my wrist. "No, I'll take a kiss."

"That isn't on the table."

"You're promising to make me king, which has to mean you're my mate. Surely one little kiss won't kill you?"

"I'd rather wait." I tried to make it sound coy, but I'm not sure it came out that way.

He laughed. "Fine, I'll take the bracelet. Let me call my father and my advisors." If Cade wasn't an heir, I'd be worried, but I was offering what he wanted on a silver platter—he had no reason to screw with me. Anyway, I had to be brave. Jess could be going through a lot worse.

He pulled out his phone and explained the situation in a few words before hanging up. "They'll be right up. Relax and enjoy your wine, you've barely touched it." He leaned back against the couch, putting an arm behind me.

I finally gave in and took a big swig of wine. "My life is insane."

He laughed. It wasn't a mean laugh, it was light. "I'm sure it's been an interesting few months."

"You could say that."

"Mind if I get some of that tension out of your shoulders?" He put a hand on my shoulder. "I hate seeing such a beautiful woman so uptight."

"You want to give me a back rub?"

He grinned. "I'd prefer to give you a full body massage, but I'm guessing I'll have to wait for that privilege."

"Privilege? Giving me a massage would be a privilege?"

"Touching you in anyway would be. To think you're holding back that kiss from me…it's killing me." He ran a finger over my lips. The intimate contact felt wrong in every way.

"Yes, I'm depriving you of one of life's greatest pleasures."

"You are." His eyes widened. I could practically feel the lust rolling off him. "So what about that backrub?"

"I think I'll pass." I resisted the urge to scoot away, that wouldn't help my cause. It was far from over. I'd have to wait it out.

He chuckled. "Were you this hard on Levi, too?"

"Worse—a lot worse." Even though I'd given in and kissed Levi early on, I'd made him wait all summer to sleep with me. If the Pteron lust thing was already in play, it must have been harder for him than I thought.

"It's going to be hard for him to let you go." Cade's expression softened slightly, the lust replaced by some level of sympathy.

I didn't say anything.

"We're going to have a great time together, you'll see."

I mumbled a quasi-agreement just as a knock on the door had Cade off the couch. He opened the door and ushered his father and two guys around his age in. Watching them made me think of Levi with Jared and Owen. Those three were probably on the war path against me already.

His father came right over, stopping in front of the couch. "You're choosing Cade? You've agreed to give him the crown?"

"I've agreed to make him a king if he can get my friend away from the Blackwells."

"Easy enough to do, but why not ask Levi to do it?" He looked at me skeptically. "There has to be a catch."

I stood up. I hated looking up at people when I talked. "Levi said to wait. I don't think my friend has time." I'd waited long enough.

"You're prepared to swear your oath?" Mr. Daley asked excitedly.

I nodded. "Yes."

"What consideration are you each offering?"

Cade answered for me. "She's offering her bracelet."

I unlatched it. "Yes, I'll offer this."

"And you?" Mr. Daly looked at Cade.

Cade reached into the pocket of the jacket he had slung over the back of a chair, and he pulled out a rectangular jewelry box. "I'd love to give you my ring, but for now I have something else."

I closed my eyes for a second—this was all way too much.

"You'll get that ruby off soon enough, but for now you need an emerald." He clasped a silver chain with a large emerald pendant around my neck.

Mr. Daly beamed. "Beautiful."

"So what do I have to do?" I touched the necklace. It was beautiful, but it felt incredibly wrong wearing someone else's stone. I already felt like part of the Laurent family.

Cade's father answered. "Swear in front of us of your intent."

"I swear that I'll make Cade a king if you rescue Jess." The words were easy enough to say, but I knew how significant they were. I hoped Levi would forgive me one day.

Cade locked eyes with me. "Accepted."

"How do we do it? How do we get her?" I asked, wanting to get things moving already. I had no idea how much time I had left before Levi found me.

"When do you want to do this?" Cade placed a hand on the back of the couch.

"As soon as possible. Levi's going to come looking for me, and if he finds me there's no chance I'm getting away again."

"How'd you get away to begin with?" He examined the pendant he'd just put around my neck.

"You don't want to know." I didn't want to imagine what my next encounter with Levi would be like. Slipping out on Jared and another Pteron guard was bad, really bad.

"I take it you want to come to New York with us?" Cade walked around the room, tossing things into a bag.

"Of course."

"Well, there's no way I'm leaving you in New Orleans anyway."

I nodded. "I understand that. I have a bag packed in my room upstairs. Could someone get it for me?"

"Yes, but we'll leave immediately."

"That's perfect." I tried to make my words sound calm, but I was terrified.

Chapter Sixteen

The only time I'd flown with a Pteron other than Levi was when Jared saved me from the cougars. The thought of flying with Cade had my stomach in knots.

"We can't just walk out the front door. The Laurents have the place surrounded." Cade hurriedly packed a few things. "Someone saw you enter, they'll be up here if we don't leave now."

I should have thought of that possibility. Even if I wasn't spotted, Levi would have the hotel searched. Running from Levi was supposed to be behind me, yet here I was doing it again. "I know."

I waited as Cade fully unbuttoned his shirt and slipped it off his shoulders. He was as muscular as I expected. I hated my reaction. I hated that I was attracted to anyone else. I shook myself.

"Glad to know you like what you see." He laughed. "You'll be seeing a lot more soon."

A shiver ran through me at his words, and I forced my eyes back up to his face.

He stepped toward me, and put a hand under my chin. "Listen, my beautiful Allie, it's going to be okay. You don't have to go anywhere near Toby."

"Yes, I do. I need to be there."

"Stubborn. She's perfect for you." Cade's father laughed. He was by far the nicest of the Pteron patriarchs I'd met. Still, I knew enough to realize he could be dangerous—very dangerous.

One of the unnamed friends pushed aside the blinds. "You need to move, Cade."

"Let's do this."

I waited for his wings to extend. I stepped back in surprise. "They're blue and gray." They were also a slightly different shape.

"What?" Cade looked at me funny. "Did you think all Pterons were part crow? We're peregrine falcons."

"Oh...I had no idea." Wow, that was news. Yet another thing Levi hadn't told me.

Cade stepped toward me. "Levi's kept you in the dark."

"I discover that more and more every day."

"I'm sure he has his reasons..." Cade moved behind me as I neared the balcony. "I'm sure you've done this before, but close your eyes if you get dizzy."

I nodded, sure he could feel the movement against his chest.

He jumped off, and I took his advice, shutting my eyes tight. I wondered what would happen if a Laurent noticed us. This was my only chance. My head swam, and I felt sick. If I were standing up, I would've fallen down.

"Shh, it's going to be okay." Cade's whispered words soothed me, and I was vaguely aware of losing consciousness.

***

I felt something cold on my head while a warm hand held mine. I opened my eyes to find myself in Cade's arms. I felt around, and my hand made contact with black leather. Cade had a cold compress on my head. "Where are we?"

"On our jet. We'll be in New York soon."

Jet? My first time on a private jet and I'd been passed out. It also reminded me of how much danger I was in. If I couldn't stay conscious with the Blackwells, I could be in a lot of trouble. "What happened?"

"You passed out." He looked worried. "Is this something that happens a lot?"

"It never used to." The truth was I had been feeling out of sorts for weeks. Something was seriously going on with my body.

Cade adjusted me in his arms. "I don't want to leave you in this condition. It's too dangerous."

"Leave me?" I fought to clear away the remaining fog of sleep.

"Do you know where Jess is?"

"No. All I know is that she's in a house somewhere near the city. Don't you know?"

Cade set aside the compress. "I'm glad you have such faith in me, but we have no idea."

"Then what's the plan? You made it sound like you could help." I struggled to sit up.

"I don't like the only solution we can come up with."

"You want to use me as bait." The realization was one I expected—I'd been banking on it.

"I'll say it again." He finally released me enough that I could sit up and lean back against the seat. "I don't want to leave you in this condition."

"You said it yourself. We don't have another choice." I was done waiting around for someone else to save Jess. It was time I did my part.

"We'll be watching you the whole time. You'll be safe."

"I'm not worried for myself. Toby won't hurt me." I was sure of it. Aside from our history, he had nothing to gain by hurting me.

"Do you really believe you're up for it?" He ran a hand through his hair.

"I don't have a choice."

"Once we retrieve your friend, we're going to make you better."

"So what now?"

"You call Toby, set up a time to meet him."

"Once we find Jess, you'll get her and her boyfriend out safely?" I needed more assurance. This had to work.

"Of course. We'll get them into hiding until the threat has passed."

"Wait, what? Hiding?" I already knew getting Jess out wouldn't be enough. She, and everyone else I cared about, wouldn't be safe until I could fix the bond with Levi. I couldn't think that big picture. The first step was to get Jess out.

"It won't be for long," Cade assured me. "We'll come up with a long term solution."

"Do you think my half-bond with Levi has anything to do with me being sick?" I hated calling our connection that. I also hated asking Cade's opinion on it, but I needed answers. I couldn't figure out why else I kept getting sick.

He shrugged. "It's a supernatural bond and it's not done right—that can't be good for a human."

"Yet another reason I need to fix this."

"Here, take this." He slipped a cell phone into my hand.

"A phone?" I examined the black and silver case. It wasn't nearly as colorful as the light blue one that held my phone.

"We couldn't take yours—Levi would have tracked you."

"Oh. I guess it's good I still remember Toby's number."

He laughed, forming a small dimple. "See, there's always a silver lining."

"So what am I saying exactly?"

"Set up a time to meet him. Then you tell him you need to see Jess before you do anything else."

"Sounds simple enough." I crossed my legs and prepared myself before dialing the still familiar number.

"Hello?" Toby picked up after three rings. His response was tentative. It took me a moment to remember that he'd have no way of knowing it was me.

I swallowed. "It's me."

"Allie? Where are you calling from?" His voice was tense—he was worried.

"A borrowed phone." That much was true. "I got a ride to New York. I need to see you."

"What? Where are you? Who gave you the ride?"

"I can't go into details. Can you meet me at that coffee shop we used to go to on Madison?"

"Of course," he responded quickly. "When?"

I glanced at Cade. I hadn't thought that part through. He mouthed "six."

"Six o'clock."

"I'll be there. Be careful." I heard the doubt in his voice. He was wondering if anything I'd told him was true. He had every reason to doubt me.

***

I gripped the side of the table for support. I couldn't believe I was actually doing it. I was willingly walking into the lion's den. I sipped my now cold coffee, trying to look like I was actually at the coffee shop for a legitimate reason. When we landed in New York, I'd stalled as long as possible. I changed out of my skirt and into jeans. Considering the icy temperature, I was grateful for that decision. I kept telling myself it was just Toby—but I knew that wasn't true. This wasn't the same guy I dated in high school. Whoever that was, was not a Pteron heir. Hopefully, he'd be in a good mood when he finally got to the coffee shop. I'd already been waiting fifteen minutes.

"Ms. Davis?"

I looked up to see two large guys wearing matching gray suits approach my table. They stopped on either side of me, effectively boxing me in. It brought back unwanted memories of being cornered in a Dairy Queen months before. I took a deep breath. It would be different this time. I was going willingly.

"Yes." I needed to put on a brave face. I was supposed to be doing this because I wanted to.

"Would you please come with us?" One of the large men spoke.

I nodded, aware that everyone around me was staring. I didn't want to know what they all thought I was doing.

I stood up, grabbing my coffee to toss it in the trash. Even if I was about to do the stupidest thing in my life, I wasn't going to leave trash on the table.

The men escorted me outside to where a black SUV sat parked against the curb. I waited for one of the guys to open the door before sliding in. The door closed behind me, and I knew with complete certainty that I'd find it locked if I tried to open it. I stayed calm—I knew Cade and his men were watching me, and losing me wasn't in their interest. I spent entirely too much time relying on others for my wellbeing.

"Where's Toby?" I asked as soon as we pulled away. I watched the coffee shop disappear through the tinted windows.

"You'll see him soon."

"I want to see him now. I'm here for Toby."

The guy in the passenger seat turned around with a grin on his face. "We're well aware who you're here to see. I assure you, he's even more eager to see you."

"Where are you taking me?"

"To Toby."

"Why didn't he meet me himself?" Alarm bells were going off. Why hadn't he met me himself? Maybe my plan wasn't going to work.

"He has more romantic plans for the two of you," the driver mumbled.

"Romantic? Toby?" I didn't bother to keep the disbelief out of my voice. I definitely wouldn't have used that word to describe him.

The passenger laughed. "What, he wasn't romantic enough for you? Is that why you dumped him?"

"You don't know anything about my relationship with Toby."

"You don't recognize us, do you?" He grinned.

"Huh? Should I?"

"I guess you were pretty wasted the last time we met."

"Excuse me?"

"Hi, Allie. It's great to finally meet the girl Toby keeps talking about," the passenger said in an exaggerated drawl.

"What? Toby's cousins?" I felt a wave of horror roll through me, remembering how I met Toby's older cousins one night when I was over at his house while his dad was away. They'd walked in on us fooling around and as they said, I'd been drunk.

"Ding ding ding. Our little cousin's been crazy since you left him. We were close to going down to New Orleans to drag you home."

"So you are actually his cousins?"

"Yes, well distant cousins, but it's all the same."

"But you're not from Texas?" I might have been drunk when we met, but I remembered their accents, and the cowboy hats.

He shook his head. "Nope. We're from Jersey."

I didn't care enough to ask why they told me the Texas story the first time. I'm sure they had their reasons.

"So you promise you'll really take me to him?" I didn't want to admit how terrified I was of facing his grandfather.

"Yes. I promise. Why would anyone keep you from him? If you don't become his mate, we don't get power."

"Good point."

"You can relax. You'll be in his bed tonight."

My stomach tightened. I had no idea how I was going to keep up the act without actually sleeping with him.

Having sex with anyone but Levi was definitely not on the table.

"Can you at least tell me where you're taking me?"

"No, but it's not too far." The driver hit his horn. I loved the city, but hated the noise. Part of me longed to be out at Georgina's. There was something so peaceful about the open landscape.

I leaned back against the seat, eventually giving in and closing my eyes. I was exhausted—more exhausted than I ever remembered feeling, and my head was gearing up for another round of pain. Hopefully, I'd manage to get through the day in one piece. I let sleep take me when I couldn't fight it anymore.

Chapter Seventeen

My door was ripped open before the SUV had come to a complete stop. "Allie." Toby nearly fell on top of me as he unbuckled my seatbelt. I'd had enough of guys messing with my seatbelt.

I sat forward, ready to get out. "Hey, Toby."

He took my hand. "I am so glad you came to your senses."

"Me too." I let him help me out.

"I'll take it from here. Thanks for getting her." Toby barely acknowledged his cousins.

"Sure, what else did we have to do?" the passenger said sarcastically. He was definitely the more talkative of the two. I still didn't remember their names, but it wasn't high on my list of priorities at the moment.

Toby barely glanced at him. "I'm sure you're being paid, so don't complain."

The talkative one laughed. "Have fun, cuz."

"I will." He opened the passenger door of his Audi SUV.

I buckled my seatbelt before he could attempt it, or anything else along those lines. "I didn't expect to be in this car again so soon…"

"No jumping out of the car on me this time." He smiled, and he seemed more like the Toby I knew. I wasn't sure if that was a good or bad thing.

"I'll try not to, if you try not to drive me crazy."

"Me? I'd never drive you crazy, unless you mean a good crazy." He winked.

"A good crazy?"

"Yeah. Don't pretend you don't remember exactly what I'm talking about." His expression heated.

I slid in my seat, moving closer to the door. "Where are we going?"

"Can't you guess?" He started the ignition.

"No…"

"You're the one who brought it up the other day." He smiled.

That's when I really looked around at where we were. I hadn't recognized the parking lot, but I definitely recognized where we were.

"Are we going back to your house?"

"Kind of."

It was surreal watching the familiar streets of my childhood fly by me. So much had changed since I'd last seen my town. I wanted to scream at Toby to take me to see my mom, but that would probably only put her in more danger.

Before I could talk myself into begging, we pulled into the driveway of Toby's childhood home. I glanced up at the large brick house—I'd spent so much time there in high school.

"I'm guessing your dad's away?" I unbuckled my seatbelt and grabbed the bag I had stowed by my feet.

"When isn't he?" Toby got out and met me at my door.

I wasn't surprised when we walked past the front door and around to the back of the house.

"Are we really climbing into the old tree house?" It was closer to the size of a studio apartment than a child's playhouse, but it was old and rustic. We'd spent hours in that tree house on the rare occasions that his dad was home.

"I can always fly you up there." He grinned. It was the big toothy grin he seemed to only use around me.

Guilt surged through me, but I pushed it down. I had a job to do. "I'll manage the climb."

He waved me on. I reached for the old rickety ladder, hoping I could come up with the right words to convince him to show me where Jess was.

"Whoa." I nearly fell backwards when I saw how he had the old wooden structure set up. Before I could really take it in, he'd come up behind me.

"I thought we could use some ambiance," he whispered in my ear.

I continued inside and he followed right behind me. For the second time in twenty-four hours, a guy who wasn't my boyfriend lit candles for me. If I weren't in my current Pteron magnet situation, this would have thrown up serious relationship red flags.

"Is that champagne?" I took a seat on one of the plush, white cushions he had set up on the floor.

"It's a night to celebrate, isn't it?"

I let out a deep breath. It was go time.

"Please tell me I'm not wrong about the celebration, Allie." He wrung his hands.

"You're not. Well, not entirely."

"What does that mean?" He kneeled down in front of me.

"I need to see Jess."

"She's fine." He ran a hand through my hair. It didn't take him long to fall back into the usual intimacies.

"How do I know that?" I sat up as straight as possible. If the ceilings were higher, I would have stood up.

"What if I let you talk to her?"

"You told me that if I came to you willing, you'd let her go."

"That was before my grandfather got involved…"

"Damn it, Toby, let her go. She has nothing to do with this."

"Once I'm king, we'll let her go. You have my word."

Yelling wouldn't help anything, I lowered my voice. "Let me see her. I need to see her."

"Tomorrow…tonight should be about us." He leaned forward, pushing me down against the cushion. "I need you, Allie."

I shook my head. "Not until I see her. I have to know she's okay."

"She's fine." He leaned over me. I could feel his breath on my face.

I pushed against his chest. I only had one more card to play. "You're forgetting one important thing, Toby. This isn't your choice. It's mine. Take me to see Jess."

He sighed, but moved off me. "We're picking up where we left off when we get back."

I mumbled noncommittally, but that must have been enough for him because he moved away.

I helped him blow out all the candles he'd just lit. "How far away is she?"

"Not far." There was something mischievous about the smile he gave me.

"Okay…"

"Want to fly there?"

"No."

He laughed. "That was fast. I'd have thought you'd like flying."

I did. With Levi. "I'd rather drive."

"You are going to fly with me eventually."

"Maybe."

"You will." He gestured for me to climb down first.

I climbed down two thirds of the way and then jumped. Toby jumped down from the top.

"Show off."

He laughed. "I'd do better than that if I were showing off."

"Let's go."

I booked it around the house and got in the car as soon as Toby unlocked the doors.

Toby got in and started the engine. "Anxious?"

"Of course, I'm anxious."

"Like I told you, it's not far." He backed out of the drive. I stared out the window at the passing houses. I knew some of the people who owned them, but not all. I wondered if they had any idea they had a neighbor who wasn't human.

"You have to be kidding me." My jaw dropped when Toby pulled into the driveway of a yellow suburban home a few blocks from his own.

"I told you it was close."

"She's been held at her own house? Where is her family?"

He pointedly looked away. "Her mom got a job opportunity she couldn't refuse. The family went ahead before selling the house."

I grabbed his arm. "Why didn't Jess tell me?"

"She just found out the day our men moved in with her."

"This is insane."

"Wishing you'd figured it out on your own? Wondering if you could have rescued her sooner?"

He knew exactly what I was thinking. He also sounded like Pteron Toby again. What was with the multiple personalities? It was like he was only himself when he thought he was about to sleep with me. I wondered how much of it had to do with me being an enchantress.

"Ready to see her?"

"Yes." I threw open my door and headed to the front steps.

"Easy there." He gripped my arm. "I should probably go first."

Before he reached the door, it was thrown open.

"We're here for a visit." Toby pulled me inside the house before the door was closed behind me.

Two men I'd never seen were seated on the couch. They were both wearing jeans and t-shirts and had their feet up on the ottoman like it was their place. It was so wrong. This was Jess' house. It was supposed to be full of little kids running around.

I turned to the men. "Where's Jess?"

"They're downstairs."

"In the basement?"

Toby swiped a chip from a bowl on the side table. "You make it sound like a dungeon. That basement is nicer than half the apartments in New York City."

I stepped away from Toby. "Someone unlock that door now."

"What do you say, boss?" one of the guys asked.

Toby nodded. "Go ahead."

One of the guys got off the couch and did it, but only after Toby nodded. I didn't care, I was so close. I wondered when the Dalys were going to act.

I took the stairs two at a time and found Jess and Emmett curled up on a sectional couch. Toby hadn't been exaggerating. The basement was easily the nicest spot in the house.

"Allie?" Jess set aside a book. Seriously? She was reading. Maybe Levi hadn't been crazy...

"I'm so glad you're okay." I ran over and hugged her. After weeks of worrying, it felt so good to finally see her. "I'm so sorry."

Jess held onto my sleeve. "What's going on?"

"Toby?" The surprise in Emmett's voice made it obvious he had no idea Toby was involved.

I turned back to Jess. "Do you know anything about the people who are holding you?"

"No. The only thing we knew was that it had to do with you. Is it Levi? Did he get you into trouble somehow?" It was weird hearing Jess talk to me like that. Like I was the one with bad judgment. It was usually the other way around.

"Something like that." I struggled to figure out what to say next, but I was spared from having to think about it for long.

The loud noises from upstairs tipped us off first, but it was the door being thrown open that made Cade's presence known. Smoke filled the basement as a booming explosion sounded.

Toby wrapped his arms around me, and I knew he had no clue what was happening as loud sounds from above us permeated the air.

I was suddenly jerked from Toby's arms. As the smoke cleared, I wasn't surprised to find myself in Cade's grasp. "Let's get out of here."

I shook my head. "Not yet."

He growled. "We've lost the element of surprise. Blackwell reinforcements are coming."

"Where's Jess? Emmett?"

"We got them. We need to go." His hand tightened on my arm.

"I'm staying."

"What?" Cade pulled me back against him. "Not a chance."

"I'm staying." I elbowed him in the chest and spun out of his arms.

I took a step back, right into Toby's arms. Without hesitation, he wrapped his arms around my waist. Surprised or not, he knew what he wanted. "I'm staying with Toby."

Cade scowled. "You made a promise. A sworn oath."

"I will keep my promise." I looked Cade square in the eye, hoping he'd understand I wasn't lying to him.

He did. "If you think it's best." Wow, Levi probably would have made me work so much harder.

"You're really not going with him?" Toby asked from behind me. He hadn't released me. I took that as a good sign.

"I'm staying with you."

"Then let's go." A loud crash upstairs made it clear more Blackwells had arrived. Toby didn't stay around to catch up with his family. He towed me to his car like he thought I was going to change my mind.

"Where are we going?" It didn't take long to realize we weren't heading back to the tree house.

"To a place up state."

"I'm sorry." I was saying those words so often now.

"For sending the Dalys after me?" He didn't take his eyes off the road.

"I didn't send them after you. I sent them to get Jess."

"Why? Why not Levi? What the hell did you promise Cade? He isn't someone to play around with, Allie."

"It doesn't matter."

His hands tightened on the wheel. "Of course it matters."

"All you need to know is that it has no bearing on why I'm with you."

He groaned. "Way to be cryptic. What other surprises do you have waiting?"

"None."

"When's Levi going to show up?"

"He's not." It hurt to say it. I missed Levi so much already.

"Likely story."

"It's true. He's not coming. He doesn't even know I'm here."

"Why? I get why you got Jess out. I get that you didn't trust I'd really let her go, but why stay with me?"

"Because it wouldn't really have ended. Yeah, Jess is free but what about my family? You know your grandfather won't give up."

"But he'll have no choice but to stop if I'm king..."
Toby placed a hand on my leg. It was too much like what
Levi did.

"You're taking me to see him, aren't you?"

"Yes. My grandfather wants to see you, but I promise
I'll be with you the whole time." He pulled onto the
interstate. "Besides, he won't be there until tomorrow. He
was under the same impression I was, that we were
spending the night at my dad's."

"Good. I don't want you to leave me." His
grandfather terrified me. I'd been around plenty of
Pterons, but he seemed even less human than the rest.

He took his eyes off the road for a moment to look at
me. "I'm going to take care of you. No one's going to hurt
you."

"I hope you're right..."

"It's going to be okay. We're going to be more than
okay." He took my hand.

"It's not just fear."

"What isn't?" He glanced over at me again.

"You were right about what you said the other day."
It was time to get back to work.

"What exactly was I right about?" He switched lanes,
passing a van.

"That you were my first...that means something."

He moved our hands to my leg. "Of course, it means
something...it means a lot."

I wanted to move our hands, but I couldn't. At least I
was in jeans.

"It's going to be like taking your virginity all over
again...it's going to be that new of an experience for you."

I squeezed my eyes shut. I felt sick and my head was
pounding again.

"Are you okay?"

"Yeah. I just haven't been feeling well lately."

"What kind of not feeling well?" he asked with concern.

"Headaches, dizziness, even passing out…"

"That doesn't sound like you at all. You hardly ever even get colds."

"I know…"

"Maybe it's stress. You'll be able to relax now. I'll make sure of it." He squeezed my leg.

I kicked the bag at my feet so I could stretch my legs out. "Can I ask you something?"

"Anything—as long as it's not going to upset you. I don't want you worrying while you're not feeling well."

Where was this super worried Toby coming from? He was always an attentive boyfriend—but certainly not like this. "Why did you ask me out?"

He didn't hesitate with his answer. "I wanted you to be mine."

"When did you decide that?" I turned in my seat to look at him.

"The first day of sophomore year. You sat down in the desk next to me in English, and you were wearing that white sundress. You know the one with the tiny holes?"

I laughed. "The eyelet dress?"

"I guess. Anyway, I was in a really bad mood because of my dad, and you turned to me and said 'you must have had a good summer.' I had no idea what you were talking about and asked what you meant. Do you remember what you said?"

"No… should I?"

"If you're that unhappy about being back in school, you had to have had a good summer. Then you shot me this smile, and I was gone."

I laughed. "Wow, I was so cool back then."

"You were. I couldn't concentrate after that. I spent the whole day thinking about the ways I could get you out of that dress."

"If you liked me sophomore year, why did you wait so long to ask me out?"

"Are you kidding? You were Allie Davis. You ate guys like me for breakfast."

"Very funny. You had a reputation of your own. You never said yes to anyone."

"I would have said yes to you—" His voice was low, like he was lost in thought.

"Even before I wowed you with my witty intellect?" I grinned.

He took a minute to respond. I was probably right about his mind moving somewhere else. "Uh yeah. I thought you were hot before that, especially in those tennis skirts you wore at the club...but I never let myself give it much thought. But that day in class—I knew you saw me."

"How'd you finally work up the nerve?" I unzipped my coat, the car was getting warm.

"Jess."

"Jess?" He had to be kidding.

"She caught me staring at you one day, and she told me you were into me."

"She did what?"

He grinned. "I knew she was lying, but I decided it was worth a shot. You'd just broken up with that idiot you were dating at the time."

"He was an idiot."

Toby laughed. "Do you remember what you said when I asked you?"

I nodded.

"Only if I'd take you out that night. You needed something to cheer you up."

I laughed. "You should have seen your face. It was a mix of elation and absolute panic."

"You didn't give me much time to prepare, but I think I did pretty well."

I tried to find a comfortable spot, but I just wanted to get out of the car. "Pizza and a movie at your house."

"What did you expect? I didn't have my license and my dad was away."

I smiled. "Yeah, well, you cheered me up."

"In other words, you thought I was a good kisser."

"I was impressed you didn't try anything else."

"I wasn't going to push my luck."

I crossed my arms. "Yeah, you were a gentleman for all of three dates. After that, you got on my back."

"You were such a tease."

"A tease?"

"Yeah. Every time I thought I was going to get lucky, you made me stop. I think we probably have the record for the most time spent naked in a bed without having sex."

"Why don't you have slits?" That reality dawned on me. I'd been with a shirtless Toby a million times. How had I never noticed it?

"Wing slits? I have them."

"Really? How did I not notice them?"

"They're not visible, and they would only feel like tiny bumps."

"Levi's are visible..." I still remembered the first time I saw them. I couldn't believe wings could come out of something so small.

He squeezed my leg again. "I'm not Levi."

"I know."

"Any more questions?"

"What color are your wings?"

"Brown. Already excited to see them?"

"Shouldn't I be?" I needed to start flirting again. "Are they big?"

"Yeah...they're bigger than Levi's crow wings. You'll see them soon." He arched an eyebrow.

"I can see your wings without having sex with you."

"Technically, yes, but it would be more fun to do it during sex."

"I want to see them before." I slipped off my jacket.

"Are you hot? I only have the heat on for you."

"Yeah. I'm still not feeling well."

"Why don't you take a nap? It's going to be another few hours."

"I think I will."

I leaned my head back against the warm leather seat and closed my eyes.

***

"Wake up, sleepyhead," Toby cooed in my ear.

"Are we there?" I opened my eyes slowly, trying to adjust to the darkness.

"We're here." He shut off the engine and got out.

I'd just unbuckled my seatbelt when he opened my door. "I'm guessing those boots aren't actually made for snow?"

"Snow? Who said anything about snow?" Were we really that far north? There hadn't even been a flurry close to the city.

He laughed. "There's quite a bit on the ground."

He was right. I must have slept for hours to have driven that far. "My boots will be fine." It couldn't be too long of a walk to the front door.

"If you say so." He held out a hand, and I used it to get down.

I slipped as my feet touched the ground. He caught me. "You said it was snow. This is ice."

"Ice covered snow."

"Great."

"Want me to carry you?"

He was too much like Levi, always offering to carry me like it was nothing. "Just hold my arm."

Toby was smart enough to realize that I wanted him to hold my weight but let me feel like I was doing it on my own.

We reached the front porch, and he unlocked the door without letting go of my arm.

I followed him right inside. I was ready to get out of the cold and was completely exhausted.

"Are we the only ones here?" I tentatively walked into the dark corridor.

"Yes. No one's going to bother us tonight." I reached out for the wall. What was taking Toby so long to turn on the lights?

I was about to turn when I was pushed into the wall. He pinned me against it, his arms on either side of me. "Why are you so nervous?"

"It's dark. Please turn on the lights, Toby." His lips brushed against my earlobe, and I forced myself not to cringe.

"I can see perfectly."

"Please, Toby, turn on the lights."

"What's the hurry?"

I didn't get a chance to answer.

Chapter Eighteen

I tried to roll over, but I couldn't move. I struggled, finally opening my eyes. I was cocooned in a strong set of arms and legs. Levi always slept with me that way, but something was off.

"You awake, baby?"

My chest clenched. It wasn't Levi.

I struggled harder, and the arms loosened. I couldn't see him in the darkness, but I was sure Toby could see me.

"What? How did we get here?" My voice was hoarse, I needed water.

"You passed out on me. You didn't even wake up when I undressed you."

"Undressed me?" I ran my hands over my body. I was still wearing my clothes.

"Gotcha."

"You mean you didn't want to take advantage of me while I was sleeping?" I croaked.

Toby figured out what I needed, and he pressed a glass of water into my hands. My eyes were gradually adjusting, and I could at least make out the glass and its contents. "Well, you probably would be more comfortable without the clothes, but…"

I gulped down the entire glass. "I don't sleep naked."

He ran a hand down my cheek. "I know for a fact that isn't always true."

"Sleeping naked after sex is different."

"It's a good thing we'll be having sex every night then, isn't it?" His hand left my cheek and moved down my neck. I wanted to recoil, but I couldn't.

"I'm not having sex tonight."

"I assumed that. I don't want our first real time together to be when you don't feel well."

"How thoughtful."

"I'm always thoughtful." He took my empty glass.

"Ow." My head pounded. What the heck was going on? If I were back home, my mom would have dragged me to a doctor already.

"When did this start?" He took my hand.

"The physical stuff? It's been getting worse the past few weeks. It's been ten times worse today."

"You were with Levi last night?"

"Yes." Had it really only been the night before?

Toby sighed. "All right, try to sleep. We'll figure this out in the morning."

"Thanks."

"I'm here for you. I always have been, and I will be for as long as you let me." Those were not the words of someone who believed their ex had come back to them.

***

"I'm taking you to him." Toby sat on the edge of the bed watching me. I was hot, oppressively so.

"Who? And why's it so hot in here?" I struggled to pull my sweater over my head. I still had a tank top on underneath.

He helped pull off my sweater and set it down next to us on the bed. "Levi. I'm taking you to Levi."

"Why?"

He let out a deep breath. "Come on, Allie. You're sick. You only got more sick when you started spending time with Cade and with me. You need Levi."

"You think it's related?"

"Yes. You already know that, just like you know that you're going to pick him."

"But—"

"Save your energy. You said his name like twenty times while you slept."

"Toby…" I struggled to find the right words.

"I know why you're here. You want to know how to fix your bond with Levi."

"And you're okay with that…" I attempted to sit up, but gave up, eventually relaxing back against the pillow.

"I don't want you sick. You look like hell, and you're only getting worse."

"Do you know how?" My voice was strained again.

"You have to get the ring off."

"But how?"

"You think I know?"

"You have to know. You told me you knew how we could be together."

"Of course, I did. I wanted you to pick me."

"So you have no clue how this works?" Panic filled my voice.

"I thought you did."

"Oh my god." This had been for nothing. Absolutely nothing. "You knew I didn't know. You just said you knew I was here about the ring."

"I figured it would just come to you."

"It's not coming to me."

"Obviously, but it's now a bigger problem. If we can't fix this damn bond, you're probably going to stay sick."

"You'll really take me to Levi?"

"Yes. Your life means something to me. I care about you whether you want to accept it or not."

"Can we go now?" Just thinking about being with Levi made me feel strong. The problem was that it also reminded me of how angry he was going to be. There was no sense worrying about it, what was done was done.

"When are we going?"

"As soon as I figure out how we're going to get there. Buying a plane ticket isn't exactly going to stay under the radar. My grandfather would do anything to prevent you from leaving. We have to keep this quiet."

I nodded. "Okay." I worked out exactly what I was going to say to Levi while I waited for Toby.

"Fuck." Toby rarely cursed. It had to be bad.

"What?"

"My grandfather and a few of his men are on their way." Toby let go of the curtain he had pulled back. I didn't see anything, but something had to have tipped him off.

"I thought they weren't coming yet."

"I guess my grandfather didn't trust me." He pressed the palms of his hands against his forehead. "For good reason."

"We're going to have to act like things are okay. We'll sneak out later." I wished I had the energy to muster some confidence for my words.

"You're right. He can't stay forever."

***

Toby and I had barely made it downstairs when the door banged open. "There you two are." Mr. Blackwell's words were simple, but the way he said it still frightened me. I moved closer to Toby.

"I left you a message. We need more time alone." Toby looked his grandfather in the eye.

The old man hung up his coat on a hook. His eyes never left us. "Surely you don't mind my presence."

I used my anger and fear to stay strong. "How can I choose Toby with you here?"

"Choose Toby?" He grabbed my hand. "Then why are you still wearing this?"

"Maybe if you hadn't interrupted us…" I tugged my hand from his.

"By all means, carry on then." He gestured to the stairs.

"I know how well Pterons hear."

"I assure you, it won't bother me."

Ugh. Dirty. Old. Man. "It will bother me. This isn't a little thing, it's big. I want privacy. It's only between Toby and I." I picked up Toby's hand. He squeezed mine. The worst part of all of this was that I knew it had to hurt Toby. I reassured myself that once I picked a king, Toby would be back to normal and could finally move on.

"You aren't in the position to have an opinion, Ms. Davis. Your stunt this afternoon was quite enough of a temper tantrum."

"A temper tantrum? Wanting to get my friends away from their kidnappers isn't a temper tantrum." I resisted the urge to stomp my foot. That would have just played into what he was saying.

"Inviting the Dalys to partake crossed a line."

"You never would have let them go. At least not alive."

He grinned. It was an evil, horrible grin. "I see you're learning not to be so naive."

"I'm here. You can leave my family and friends alone."

He laughed. "Why would I listen to you?"

"Because you have to." I had the power—it was all about my choice.

"I don't have to do anything. I can make you do whatever I want. You just don't want to know how."

I shivered. "Are you threatening me?"

He stepped toward me. "Yes."

"Don't move any closer." Toby pushed me behind him.

"Don't tell me what to do, boy."

"Allie's going to be my mate. I'm the only one who touches her or tells her what to do." Normally I would have snapped at him implying he could tell me what to do, but he was probably acting—just like me.

"Then make her your mate. It's taking you long enough."

"I plan to, but we're doing it alone. You've seen her. Now I'm taking her home with me where we can have privacy."

"Privacy?" He laughed. "You're pathetic. Just like your father. How your mother married such a weak human, I'll never understand."

Toby bristled, but he didn't lose his temper. "We're going."

Toby didn't give me any warning. He grabbed me around the waist as he sped to the front door. I'd barely registered brown wings extending before we were airborne.

Frozen. I felt almost agonizingly cold before Toby landed.

"Damn it. I should have thought about the cold. I wish I had a coat for you."

We were in the middle of nowhere, in a forest with a thick cover of trees. Only a faint hint of light spilled through the canopy.

"I need to sit down." I fell down to my knees, wrapping my arms around myself.

"I think you're worse. You keep getting worse." He started to pace. "Do you have Levi's number memorized?"

"Yeah." I barely got the words out through my chattering teeth.

"What is it? You're too sick to travel. Maybe just being with him will help a little." Toby kneeled down next to me.

I shakily told Toby the numbers and waited for him to dial.

I wanted to lie down on the ground, but Toby held me instead.

"Levi, it's Toby."

"Just shut up. She needs you. She's sick, and I have no freaking clue what else to do."

He started describing our location, and I took small breaths to relax myself. I refused to pass out again.

Chapter Nineteen

"What did you do to her?"

Levi landed in the clearing and immediately pulled me into his arms. I closed my eyes as I waited for my headache to subside.

"What did I do to her? This is all your fault." Toby paced back and forth. We were still in some random forest somewhere.

"My fault?" Levi held me tightly against him. Despite how weak I felt, there was something so comfortable about being tucked in his arms. "What do I have to do with it? She was fine when I last saw her."

"It's your messed up bond that has her sick. If you weren't so stupid, you'd have figured it out already."

"How the hell did you even get her? I thought she was with Cade." Levi's whole body tensed. Talking about me being with two other heirs wasn't easy for him.

"Like you didn't know. We knew you had the house under surveillance."

Levi shifted, his shoes crunching the fallen leaves covering the forest floor. "It shorted out a few hours ago."

"You knew Jess was at her own house?" I had to get the words out. If it had been that simple, he should have just told me.

He looked down at me. "Allie? You're awake."

"Yes, I'm awake." I kept the part about feeling like hell to myself.

Toby continued to pace. "Don't make her waste energy. You have to fix this."

"Is it really that simple?" We all turned as Cade walked into the clearing where we waited, as though Levi and Toby in the same place wasn't bad enough.

"What the hell are you doing here? I thought Allie made it clear she wasn't interested." Toby's eyes darkened.

Cade stepped closer. "She also made me a promise."

"A promise?" Levi asked suspiciously.

"Yes." Cade looked right at Levi. "She's picking me."

"No. There's no way Allie would do that." Levi's voice wavered and he purposely avoided looking down at me.

I made myself speak. "I promised to make him a king, but it's not what you think."

"No." Levi shook his head. "No."

Cade stepped toward where Levi still held me. "She gave a sworn oath. I have witnesses."

"What?" Levi's entire body shook, and I knew that if I could see his eyes, they'd be black.

Toby jumped in. "He can't hold her to anything she said when she was sick."

Cade crossed his arms. "She wasn't sick when she said it."

Levi didn't say anything at first, and that scared me. I wanted to explain, but I couldn't do it yet. Finally, I felt his body relax slightly. "Not another word. No one's accomplishing anything if she's unconscious. We have to help her first. We'll discuss this issue later."

Cade sighed, like he was realizing he didn't have any other choice. "We should talk to your grandmother. If anyone can help, it's Georgina."

I wished. "She doesn't know how."

"She has to." Toby said it like it had to be fact.

"She's the one who suggested I flirt with you to find out how."

"With me?" Toby pointed at his chest. "She thought I'd know?"

"Yes. Evidently you fooled us both."

"If she doesn't know, she'll know someone who does," Levi said it resolutely. "I'll take Allie to see Georgina right now."

"I'm coming." Toby stepped toward us.

"Me too." Cade mimicked Toby's motion.

Levi shook his head. "We don't need you slowing us down."

Toby bristled. "As if we'd slow you down. I don't think she's in the shape to fly."

"Obviously not. I'll get us a ride." Levi shifted me in his arms so he could get to his phone. I waited while he spoke to someone. He hung up. "Let's head to the road."

***

Nestled in the backseat of a car with my head in Levi's lap, I tried to comprehend what was happening. I was driving across the country with three Pteron heirs to talk to someone who already told me she had no idea how to help. For the first time, I was scared for myself. This wasn't just feeling under the weather. The headaches were one thing, but overwhelming exhaustion and passing out was another. There was something seriously wrong with me.

"It's going to be okay." Levi's words did little to soothe me, but his hand resting on my chest helped. In the past few months, I'd grown so close to him, I couldn't even stand the thought of having to say goodbye.

"I love you." Getting words out was becoming harder, but those were too important to leave unsaid. I couldn't explain myself to him until we had time alone. I had a feeling that wouldn't be happening for a while.

"Georgina still hasn't called back?" Cade asked from the driver's seat. Levi had fought Toby off when he tried to get in the back seat with us. He'd settled for sitting sideways in the passenger seat so he could watch me. I must have dozed off when Levi called his grandmother, because I couldn't recall the conversation.

Levi gently stroked my stomach through my sweater. "She said it could take a few hours to make contact."

"Does she realize how serious the situation is?" Toby still hadn't turned around.

"Of course, she does. She promised she'd be ready for us when we got there."

I sighed loudly.

"Are you still awake, Allie?" Cade asked. "You should probably try to get some sleep."

Having three grown men worrying about me wore me out. Sleep would probably be a welcome distraction. I closed my eyes and concentrated on the feel of Levi's hand.

I spent the entire ride fading in and out of consciousness. One great thing about Pterons is that they don't need to sleep much, so we drove through the night. The sun shone through the window when we pulled into Georgina's drive.

"Where is she?" Georgina yelled loudly enough that I could hear her through the closed window.

She pulled open the car door before Levi could open it himself. "Take her inside, now."

Levi stepped out of the car without setting me down. "Did you find someone who can help?"

"Of course I did, Leviathan. Quit wasting your breath on such pointless questions." Despite my state, I had to smile. I'd never heard anyone talk to Levi that way. I'd also never heard anyone call him by his full name other than at formal events.

Georgina didn't bother to acknowledge the other guys. It didn't surprise me at all. A servant held the door open, and Levi carried me inside to a sitting room down the hall from the screened in porch.

"Is this the girl?" A tiny old woman asked when Levi walked us into the room.

Georgina nodded. "Yes. This is the next queen. Do whatever it takes."

A cold hand touched my arm as the old woman examined my hand. "How long has this ring been on?"

"Since August, Mayanne." Georgina didn't give Levi a chance to answer.

"Your grandson is the one who bungled the bond?"

"Bungled it—" Levi started to say before Georgina cut him off.

"Yes, she's my grandson's mate. What I care about is fixing it."

"It can't be fixed," Mayanne said flatly.

"What? Why are we wasting our time here if she can't help?" Toby yelled.

The old woman glared at Toby. "Calm yourself, boy. It can't be fixed, but it can be undone. First we need to get her strength back."

"How do we do that?" Levi still cradled me against his body. I held on to consciousness by running my fingers down his chest. "And who are you?"

"My name's Mayanne. I knew your great-grandmother Carol well."

Levi shifted me slightly. "Are you a witch?"

"Yes," she said resolutely.

"Can we trust her?" Levi asked Georgina.

"Absolutely."

Levi sighed. "We don't have any other choice..."

"No, you don't." Mayanne grabbed a large tote bag. "I need to make a drink. Georgina, please assist me in the kitchen."

"Very well."

The two women left the room.

"A drink? You don't think she means liquor, do you?" Toby asked no one in particular.

Cade laughed dryly. "I'd hope it's more than that. Besides, how would that get her strength back? It would just make her more tired." He crossed his arms and turned to Levi. "You could sit down you know. You don't have to play the hero and hold her all day."

"It's not like she's heavy. I prefer standing." Levi didn't sound like himself, and that worried me. He was always the one who stayed strong.

I snuggled my head into his shirt. Staying awake was probably more work than Levi was using to hold me.

Georgina and Mayanne returned before I could drift off again.

"Drink this." A cold glass was pressed against my lips.

"Wha?" I tried to ask.

"Don't waste your energy. Just drink it." Mayanne was surprisingly forceful for such a small woman. Still, I wasn't going to drink something without knowing what it was.

I shook my head.

"Just drink it, babe. It's going to make you better." Levi put his hand on top of mine.

"I never said it would make her better. I said it would make her strong enough to get through what she has to get through."

"It's safe, Allie." Georgina appeared next to me.

I nodded. For one reason or another, I really trusted her. I opened my mouth and let the cold, bitter drink spill down my throat. There was something familiar about the taste.

Mayanne must have read my expression. "It's pomegranate juice. That's what you're tasting."

"Pomegranate juice? That's your great idea?" Toby fumed.

Mayanne smiled, and her whole face lit up. "Natural antioxidants have a lot of healing properties."

Georgina laughed. "There's more than pomegranate juice in there, but that's all Allie needs to know about."

I wanted to regurgitate the drink. What was I drinking?

"It may take up to an hour."

"Were you being serious? Is it really that dangerous?" Levi finally sat down. I clung to him.

He leaned down to whisper in my ear. "Even if you let go, I'm not putting you down."

I smiled, but the next words out of Mayanne's mouth wiped that smile away immediately. "An improper bond is lethal."

Levi hung his head. "I'm such an idiot."

"Glad you finally admit it." Toby was back to his pacing again.

"How does it work? You said there was something we could do." Levi sounded calmer. More resolute.

"The one who made the improper bond has to undo it. You have to repeat the same sequence of events that led to Allie receiving the ring, and you have to ask for it back."

"Ask for it back?" His voice shook. My chest ached.

Mayanne nodded. "Yes. That's essential. You need to take the ring back, and you have to do it in exactly the same way you gave it to her. Same place, same time, same clothes."

"How do you know this is going to work?"

"I don't…but it's the only possibility I know of."

"How do you even know? Where is this information from?" Toby sat down on the arm of the sofa.

"I can't give you all the details. All I can say is that Allie's great-grandmother taught me everything I know."

"What?" I sputtered out.

Mayanne smiled at me kindly. "That's a story for another time."

"Wait. How do you know her? Please."

"We grew up together. Save your energy." She put a hand on my forehead, and then nodded. "I think the drink is going to kick in soon."

Levi squeezed my hand before running a finger over the ring.

"You can give the ring right back to her." Georgina tried to comfort Levi.

"Like hell he will," Cade snapped. "She made a sworn oath. She's taking my ring."

"She is making her own choice this time." Toby was calmer, but I didn't doubt his determination.

After only ten minutes, I felt different—more normal. Whatever it was that Mayanne gave me was working. "How much time do we have?"

"No more than a week."

"Then we're doing it now. No sense cutting it close." Toby had finally stopped moving.

"I can't believe I'm saying this, but you're right." Levi brushed some hair off my face. "As soon as Allie is up to it, we should go."

"I'm feeling better." I wasn't in a rush to separate myself from Levi, but I was tired of feeling sick. We needed to find a resolution to this whole mess.

Georgina placed a hand on my shoulder. "Why don't you rest upstairs for an hour or so, Allie. The boys can wait down here."

"That sounds good." I knew I could probably walk, but I let Levi carry me upstairs to the room we were supposed to stay in the last time we were there.

"I'm staying with you." Levi stretched out next to me on the bed.

"Levi, I promise I'm not trying to hurt you or us. I had a reason for everything, and it's going to work out."

"I'm not letting you go." He didn't say anything else before pulling me into his arms so we could sleep.

Chapter Twenty

We made sure to get every detail right. I even changed in my room at the hotel. Levi had Hailey find "the dress" and she brought it over. I could still remember how excited I'd been the last time I put on the black, lacy dress—and how eager I was when Levi took it off. I tried to fight back the tears I knew were threatening to spill, but I couldn't.

"You're going to be okay. He'll give it back." Hailey's words helped, but she didn't know everything. I hadn't told her about the deal with Cade. It had been hard enough facing her.

"I wanted this ring off so bad, but now I never want to let it go."

"Who would have thought?" She sat down on the edge of my bed as I finished my makeup in the bathroom. I wasn't sure if the makeup had to be the same, but I'd put on more that night.

"I'm sorry I didn't tell you what I was doing." The words had been on the tip of my tongue since she came over, but I hadn't found the strength to say them yet.

"I'm sorry you didn't feel like you could. I'm here for you, Allie. I would have helped you. You never have to feel alone."

Her words felt real, and I wondered if I'd made a huge mistake. I should have at least talked to Hailey before approaching Cade. I'd just been so afraid of her going to Levi. I felt so overwhelmed, and I didn't know who I could trust.

She thankfully changed the conversation. "So Georgina really trusts this Mayanne person?" Hailey was lying down by the time I finished.

I ran a hand through my hair. I had to wear it down.

"Yes, she's a witch and somehow knows my great-grandmother."

"Isn't that weird?"

"Georgina did act weird when I told her where my grandmother was from. I think it's where the other enchantresses originated. "

Hailey laughed.

"What?"

"Isn't it funny that the fate of The Society has been in the hands of random women from a tiny Russian town?"

I shrugged. "No weirder than anything else I've discovered over the last few months."

Hailey stood up. "I should go. If I'm here when Levi shows up, I could somehow mess things up, right? Like change it too much."

"You probably should even though I don't want you to."

She hugged me. "I'll see you on the other side."

I reluctantly broke the hug. "You make it sound like I'm dying."

"No...that's what would happen if you didn't do this."

I hugged her for a moment longer before letting go. "See you on the other side."

She gave me a half smile before walking out the door.

I settled down on the couch to wait. I had to pull myself together. It was going to be just as hard on Levi, if not worse. He already held himself responsible for everything that had gone wrong since giving me the ring.

I jumped at the knock on the door. I was lost in the memory of the first time I'd met Levi. There had been nothing romantic about that meeting, yet it was an event I would never forget.

"Hello there, gorgeous." Levi sent a wave of déjà vu over me.

"You don't look so bad yourself." I still remembered using that understatement. Once again, he looked incredible in his khakis and dress shirt. I wanted to jump him, not watch him break.

"Are you ready for this?" His expression fell, like he'd momentarily convinced himself this was just a date, but the reality had hit him again.

"I'll never be ready, but we don't have a choice." I looked down.

His hand moved under my chin to make me look up at him. "I love you, Allie. I love you."

"I love you, too." That's when the tears started for real. I ended up hysterical in his arms. I didn't even want to know what my makeup looked like.

He rubbed my back. "We can do this."

I nodded. "Okay. Do I need to clean up?"

He wiped away a little bit of mascara from my face. "Nope. You're prefect."

I laughed. "You'd say that no matter what I looked like right now, wouldn't you?"

"Yeah, I would because it's true."

"Don't make me cry again."

"I can't promise that." He took my hand and led us to the elevator.

I shivered when we walked outside. It was only fifty degrees out, and I was wearing a tiny dress, but Mayanne had made it clear that we needed to dress exactly the same. I could tell Levi wanted to give me his coat, but he knew he couldn't.

We were seated at the same table at Antoine's. It was in the corner, tucked away from everyone else. The first time we'd been in there, I'd been so impressed with the decor and the menu. This time, the last thing I wanted was food.

The very same waiter approached our table. I wondered how Levi had made sure of that. It couldn't have been random. Levi was taking this seriously. "Welcome to Antoine's. Can I get you something to drink?"

"Yes, a 1982 Chateau Mouton Rothschild."

"Great selection." The waiter didn't seem surprised by our order. Evidently, Levi must have called ahead to make sure they had a bottle.

Levi tasted the wine, and the waiter filled our glasses. "To a truly amazing summer and to many more celebrations." His words weren't light this time, they were hoarse.

We clinked glasses, and I sat back in my chair. I'd loved the wine the first time, but that night it tasted too dry and almost bitter.

The waiter returned and Levi ordered exactly what we'd had the first time. By the time the Oysters Rockefeller arrived, I wanted to be sick. I didn't know how much more I could take and it was only going to get worse.

"You know this dish was invented here." He was repeating our exact conversation. I tried to force myself to play along.

"Really?"

I pushed around the food on my plate knowing what was coming.

"I need to take something from you." He whispered the words.

I nodded.

"Give me the ring." Silent tears slid down Levi's face, and I broke completely. "I need it back from you. I want it back from you." I'm sure everyone in the restaurant watched us, trying to figure out why two people were crying while seemingly sharing a romantic meal. I was about to make it crystal clear.

"I want to give you the ring back." The words came to me naturally, and they burned coming out. My tears matched Levi's as I easily slid the ruby ring off my finger and placed it in his palm.

All at once, it felt like a weight had been lifted off me. I felt lighter, and my head felt clear for the first time in days. I let out a deep breath. The physical relief was in sharp contrast with the emotional toll giving the ring back had on me. Inside, I was a mess.

"How long do I have to wait before I give you my ring back?"

"Levi…"

"No. Please…you have to take it back." He was on the verge of tears again.

"I will, just not tonight. I can't do it now."

"Allie, please."

"She said no." Cade approached the table with Toby next to him.

"What are you doing here?" I asked.

"They wanted to make sure I really did it." Levi sounded lifeless, and I knew it was all because of me.

"Are you ready to do what you promised, Allie?" Cade stood right next to my chair.

"Yes, but it's not what you think."

"How is it not what I think?" he snapped.

If we were attracting attention before, we were like beacons now. "Let's talk about this somewhere else."

Levi quickly paid the bill, and we walked outside. I slipped my arms into the jacket Levi offered. The sun had gone down hours before, and a chill had set in since we left the hotel. "Thanks."

"Of course." Levi's words were soft, but his face was hard. I'd hurt him by refusing to take his ring back. I just knew it had to be done differently this time, done on my own terms.

"Should we go to the hotel?" I asked, wanting a destination even if the thought of sitting in a room with three angry Pteron heirs scared me.

"Works for me." Levi remained glued to my side.

The others agreed, and we started to head back toward the hotel. I snuggled into Levi's jacket, loving that it still smelled faintly like him.

We'd just turned the corner when all three guys tensed.

"Stay close." Levi wrapped an arm around me, and I leaned in. Something had the guys on edge.

"How many are there?" Toby said quietly.

Levi answered absently. "I don't know yet."

"What's going on—"

Cade cut me off. "Pterons."

"Pterons?" I barely whispered but I was sure they could all hear.

Toby's voice came from right behind me. "We're surrounded."

I glanced around and saw nothing but darkness. We'd taken a back way home, through a dark alley, something I didn't question considering who I was walking with. Once again, I wished I hadn't placed my safety in others' hands. I didn't see a single soul, something surprising even on the back streets of the French Quarter.

"They're yours, aren't they?" Cade spun around to face Toby.

Toby tensed. "I have no idea how they knew how to find us, I swear."

"They're your grandfather's men?" We passed under a street light, and for the first time I caught a glimpse of something moving on a rooftop.

"Yes." Toby's hands were in fists.

"Get help as soon as possible," Levi ordered Cade. "Get your men and mine."

Cade visibly stiffened. "I'm not leaving Allie with you."

"She doesn't break promises. If she promised you something, you'll get it. I'm strongest and you know it, but you're faster. Get help. That's the only way we're going to protect her."

Cade nodded before stripping off his shirt and transforming. He flew off and even in the dim lighting, I saw several other Pterons following him.

As soon as Cade left, at least a dozen transformed Pterons jumped down from the buildings above.

Levi tried to push me behind him, but more and more men emerged. We were surrounded. I searched for Toby. He was nowhere to be seen. Had he abandoned us that easily? There had to have been well over twenty Pterons. I clutched Levi's arm until my fingers were pried off at the same time I was grabbed from behind. I was too terrified to scream as I was dragged further into the alley.

Levi fought off the first few Pterons. They wriggled on the ground as he prepared to take on the next set. Then everything changed as another dozen Pterons jumped in. I watched with horror as Levi was hauled in the other direction. At least six men had to hold him back, but eventually he disappeared from my view. I let out a whimper, and I was rewarded with a hand across my mouth. If these men could take Levi, I was in serious trouble.

Struggling was no use. It was like fighting against chains. The more I squirmed, the tighter the arm held me. I eventually stopped fighting, but the arm didn't loosen. I couldn't see anything but large brown wings.

The sea of wings parted, and out of the shadows walked my nightmare, Mr. Blackwell. The wall of Pterons moved back into place behind him. "Hello again, Allison." His voice was sharp and angry.

Suddenly, the empty space next to him was filled by Toby. My body relaxed a small amount knowing he was near. Despite everything, I trusted him. "You're not touching her."

Mr. Blackwell glared at his grandson. "Like hell I'm not. She's coming with us now. You're coming too."

Toby glanced at me before looking back at his grandfather. "You can't force her to choose me."

"True, but I can make it impossible for her not too." He cracked his knuckles.

"What do you mean?" Toby took a step closer to me. The Pteron holding me dropped his hand from my mouth, but I knew better than to yell. They weren't going to give me a chance to call for help.

Mr. Blackwell turned his angry gaze on me. "It's amazing what a few days, or weeks, in a dungeon can do to someone…"

"You can't mean that! You can't treat her that way!" Toby seethed. He had moved right next to me, and I could see his already black eyes getting even less human.

"Why not? She just needs to accept your ring and let you take her. It's not too complicated, child."

Toby growled. "That's it? That's all you view her as?"

Mr. Blackwell got that evil grin again. It was dark, but I could still see his white teeth. "Well, she also needs to give you an heir, and she's the only girl you can be with so I suppose you'll have to take her more than once."

"No." Toby stepped in front of me, blocking his grandfather from my view.

Screams and grunts filled the air. I hoped that Cade had gotten help. The thought of anyone hurting Levi made me break inside. He was strong, but he couldn't take on that many Pterons alone.

"Don't forget your place," Mr. Blackwell snapped.

Toby brushed against me, and I knew it was his way of letting me know he would protect me. "I only wanted to be king so I could have Allie back. But not like this. She deserves better than this."

"This has nothing to do with what you want or what she deserves. Although, I think it's exactly what the girl deserves," Mr. Blackwell spit.

That seemed to set Toby off more. "Over my dead body."

"I wish I could do just that, but unfortunately only an heir can take power. I need you alive, for a while." Only the most evil man could say that about his grandson. But then again, Mr. Blackwell wasn't a man.

The distant noise got louder, and I knew the fight had found us. A wall of Pterons blocked the fighting from me, but I could imagine what it looked like. I hoped they were at least keeping humans away. They'd only become collateral damage.

"Take the girl, we're leaving before this mess gets worse," Mr. Blackwell directed the two men next to him. They appeared to be his body guards. Aside from the one holding me, they were the only ones watching us talk.

"I said no." Toby lunged at his grandfather, easily pushing off the guards who tried to stop him. He was stronger than I imagined. Toby wrapped his hands around the older man's throat, and I was released as my captor tried to pry Toby off. It was too late. I nearly vomited when I heard a cracking sound. Toby let go of his grandfather and the old man's lifeless body fell to the ground.

Before I'd even processed what was happening, I was grabbed from behind again. I struggled and managed to land a groin shot before he pulled me back against him. "Bitch."

"Release her!" Toby yelled, but it fell on deaf ears. Other brown-winged Pterons had figured out what happened and were surrounding Toby.

I screamed as another Pteron stepped toward me with what appeared to be a burlap sack.

Before the bag could be put over my head, the figures blocking the entrance to the alley fell back, and the Pteron I wanted more than anything stepped into view.

"Levi?"

He walked toward me with a whole line of Pterons behind him, including Jared and Owen. The rest of the Blackwell Pterons stepped back. Evidently, they were ready to surrender.

"I'm here." Levi was sweaty, with a few cuts, but otherwise he looked unharmed. "Are you okay?"

I nodded.

"Stay here." Levi moved me over to Jared, who pulled me into a near bone crunching hug. I waited as other Laurent Pterons, as well as others with blue and gray wings like Cade's, grabbed the remaining Blackwells.

"You did that to save her, didn't you?" Levi wasn't talking to me.

I tugged on Jared so he'd walk with me over to where Levi and Toby stood leaning over Mr. Blackwell's body.

Toby nodded solemnly. "He would have treated her like an animal."

"You did that to save me…" I said in awe. I couldn't believe it.

Toby wiped blood off his face. Someone had broken his nose. "I couldn't…I couldn't let him do that to you."

I hugged him. I hugged the first boy I'd ever loved. I understood it now. What we'd shared had been love, it was just different from what I had with Levi.

Jared called to Levi. "Get Allie out of here. We'll take care of the rest."

Levi hugged me, and he didn't let go for a full minute. "Thank god you're okay."

I knew I couldn't go home. There was still so much that had to be discussed, but I felt safe in his arms. I never wanted him to let go.

***

"Allie, it's time." Cade stepped into my room at the hotel. I hadn't moved from where Levi set me down on the couch next to him. I held onto his arm almost as intensely as I had on the street. This time, I was worried about someone else taking me away.

I forced myself to meet Cade's gaze. "I will keep my promise."

"Allie, no. Please," Levi begged. The desperation in his voice rocked me to the core.

I took a deep breath. "I promised Cade he could be a king if he saved Jess."

Levi's face fell. "Did you really swear an oath?"

"Yes—but."

Levi shook his head. "No."

"Let me finish. I promised he could be a king, not that I'd be his mate."

"Where's the difference, Allie? I don't see any," Cade watched me carefully. He must have gone to his room, because unlike the rest of us, he wore a clean shirt.

I sat up. "Levi has two choices."

"Me? I have choices?" Levi asked.

"Yes." I took his hands in mine. "You can either say goodbye and let me go as Cade's mate…"

"Or?" Levi looked at me hopefully. "The other one has to be a better option."

"You can have me as your mate, but give Cade a kingship." I searched his face, looking for a hint to his answer. "What about the West Coast?"

"Wait, you want to be Levi's mate but give me the West Coast?" Cade looked at me questioningly.

I nodded. It was exactly what I wanted. Not only would I get the man I loved, but it meant we'd have another family to align with. Hopefully it would mean avoiding any more of the fights I'd just witnessed. When I'd first mentioned my proposed platform to Georgina, I hadn't imagined I'd try to maneuver it the way I did, but I just knew it was what I had to do.

"Absolutely. Done." Levi nodded before pulling me back into his arms.

Cade smiled. "I'm okay with that."

"I'm not officially king yet, but I give my word." Levi shook Cade's hand.

"She already gave it…" Cade nodded at me.

I sensed there was an unspoken conversation between them, or maybe the handshake held more significance than I realized. I was too relieved to worry about it.

"I'm sure I'll be seeing you again soon." Cade kissed my hand.

I smiled. It was a real smile. "I'm sorry if I misled you."

He grinned. "I want you, but I understand. It was my fault for not seeing through your words. But anyway, my girlfriend will be thrilled about the turn of events."

"Girlfriend?"

"Yeah. I didn't even know about you until a few months ago. You are gorgeous, though. Levi's a lucky man." He winked before disappearing through the doorway.

"That was a lot easier than I expected…" I turned in Levi's arms to look at him. "Aren't you supposed to be angry?"

"The West Coast is more trouble than it's worth. My job's going to be ten times easier."

"Is that the only reason you're okay with it?" I hoped there was more.

"No. The reason I'm okay with it is because I get you." He started to kiss me, but I pushed on his chest. Toby was watching.

"I guess that's my cue." Toby looked down at the carpet.

I stood up. "I'm sorry, Toby."

He shrugged. "This sucks, but maybe when you actually become his mate, my feelings will fade, or at least the supernatural ones. I know I love you for more reasons than that."

I sighed. "Thanks for everything, Toby." I hugged him again. It was a goodbye hug, and we both knew it.

"I'd do anything for you. I wish I'd made you see that sooner, but you never looked at me the way you look at him. You probably never would have been as happy."

"Thank you." Levi nodded at Toby. "Thank you for bringing her back to me. Thank you for making such a sacrifice to protect her."

"I didn't do it for you." Toby gave me a small smile.

Levi looked lost in thought for a minute before he turned back to Toby. "Do you want a job?"

"A job?"

"You're now the head of your family." Levi stood up next to me.

"Yeah. What's your point?" Toby asked.

"Want to manage New York for me?"

Toby's eyes widened. "Like as a king?"

"No. I'm not giving up more than my princess here already has. You'd work under me in title, but you get the decision making power."

"Yes." Toby held out his hand to shake with Levi.

Toby stepped toward the door. "Be safe and be happy." He didn't give me a chance to reply before leaving Levi and I alone.

"Are you ready to go home?" Levi asked.

"Don't we have to take care of things?"

"No, I think we're good for tonight."

"Then let's go home."

***

I must have slept through the whole next day. When I woke up it was dark again, but there was enough light spilling in through the window to know we were home. "Levi?"

"I'm right here, babe." He kissed my shoulder. "I want to do something special for dinner tonight."

"Special? Please, no French food or wine." The thought of eating Oysters Rockefeller again made me sick. I never wanted to relive that experience ever again. "How about Mexican and beer? That sounds perfect."

Levi laughed. "Mexican food and beer?"

"Or sangria. Get Georgina's recipe. It's fantastic."

***

In the end, I was the one who called Georgina. She'd been thrilled to hear I was okay, and she was more than happy to share her recipe. They were just as good I remembered, and after two glasses, and some awesome Mexican food from Superior Grill, we moved into the living room. I took a seat on the couch. Levi didn't sit next to me.

"Are you okay?"

"Yes. I'm fine." He still stayed standing, shoving his hands in his pockets.

"Are you sure?"

"There's just something I've been meaning to ask you for a while." He shifted nervously.

"Yeah?"

He dropped down to one knee and my breath hitched. "Allie Davis, will you do me the greatest pleasure in the world and become my wife, and my queen?"

My heart leapt. "You're proposing?"

"Yes…" He opened his hand, the ruby ring lay on his palm.

"What happens if I say no?"

His face blanched.

"Sorry, just kidding. Yes! Of course, it's yes."

He slipped the ruby ring back on my finger, and I knew in every fiber of my body that it was never coming off again.

He sat down next to me, and I fell into his arms. "I love you."

"I love you too."

"Remember what you told me? That you kind of wished I was proposing that night?" His eyes were full of a happiness I'd only seen once before—the night in the cave.

"I actually said I thought about how I'd like it at some point." I slipped his sports coat off of him, it was in my way. He'd insisted on us dressing up a little even if it was for takeout. I now knew why.

"Same thing."

I laughed. "All right."

"This time I really did."

"Yes, you did."

He stroked my arm. "So what's next?"

"We make you king." I took his hand and led him upstairs into our bedroom. "Do you remember what you did last time?"

He put his hands on my hips. "I just made love to you with the intent to make you mine forever."

"Do it again." I started unbuttoning his shirt. "I'm doing it too."

"In a hurry?" He laughed, already unzipping my dress.

"As a matter of fact, yes, I am."

"Me too." He reached around to unclasp my bra as soon as my dress hit the floor.

I discarded his shirt before pulling his white tank over his head. "Are you as excited this time as you were the first time?"

"I'm just as excited every time." He leaned over to kiss me before picking me up and carrying me to the bed.

I unbuckled his belt and unbuttoned his pants. "Can you lie on your wings?"

"Dare I ask why you want to know?"

"I'm in control tonight. I need to be on top and you always transform."

"Sure, I can lie on them." He sat down on the bed next to me. "Especially for this reason."

I yanked off his pants and boxers just as he pulled off my panties.

I leaned over him, making him lie down on the bed. Climbing on top of him, I took a moment to think about the step I was taking. I was about to willingly tie myself to Levi. I could leave without the ring if I wanted—but leaving was the last thing on my mind.

I leaned down to kiss him. "It's really going to be forever."

He looked me right in the eye. "I can't wait."

The first time was incredible, and it had only gotten better, but that night brought things to a new level. He put his hands on my hips, and we moved together in perfect synchrony. I could think of nothing but how amazing it felt to connect with Levi, to feel so completely open and vulnerable, but also incredibly safe.

We reached our climaxes together, and I fell down on top of him, exhausted, but feeling completely alive.

"I love you," he whispered as he cradled me in his arms.

"I love you too." I didn't need to check the ring to know it wasn't going anywhere, but I did anyway.

Chapter Twenty-One

"Happy Birthday." Levi kissed my lips gently.

"Thanks, but we both know that's not the big celebration of the day." I pulled the sheets up around me, Levi had shifted away from me, leaving me cold.

He got the hint that I was cold and pulled me back into his arms. "What could possibly be more important than the birth of Allison Davis?"

I sighed contently, glad to be back in his arms. "Hmm, I don't know. Maybe your coronation?"

He laughed. It was that deep laugh he only used when he was really happy. "Your birthday is still more important. I'd have no interest in becoming king if it weren't with you by my side."

"Where did this sappy Levi come from?" I snuggled even further into his chest.

"Sappy? It's romantic, babe."

"I know."

He kissed my shoulder. "Do you think you'll ever get tired of giving me a hard time?"

"No. If I did, I'd be worried."

He laughed again. "Good to know. If I see it happening, I'll just come up with new ways to drive you crazy."

I glanced at the alarm clock. It was one of those that wakes you up with light and not noise. At first I was skeptical, but it really worked. We hadn't set the alarm the night before and were cutting it a little close. "We have to get up, don't we?" I picked up my phone from the night stand. I had a missed text from Jess. We were talking a lot again. Her life had finally returned to normal, and, thankfully, she didn't seem to hold a grudge against me. Maybe it had something to do with Emmett asking her to move in. I don't think she could be mad at anyone after that.

"Yeah, we do. But on a positive note, we still get to take a shower."

"Oh, you think you're joining me?"

"No. I know it."

"Ohhh, Mr. Confident now."

"First I'm sappy Levi, and now I'm Mr. Confident." He rolled me over on top of him.

I giggled. He made me do that so often. "I'm your mate. I'm allowed to make up as many names for you as I want."

"Mmm, there's something sexy about the way you say that. I like hearing you call yourself my mate."

"Well, it's true." I trailed a line of kisses down his chest.

"It is. You were before, but now no one can deny it."

"You say it."

He ran his hands up and down my arms. "You want me to call you my mate?"

"No, I want you to call yourself my mate, or is it not called that?"

"I've actually never heard a Pteron refer to themselves as a mate before."

"It can't go one way."

"It doesn't with us. I'm your mate, Al."

I grinned. "Now you're being Mr. I'll do or say anything to get you naked in the shower, Levi."

"You're already naked, Al."

"I am, aren't I?" I pushed off the sheets and hopped out of bed. "Glad you pointed that out."

His eyes devoured me. "Glad I'm the only one who gets to see your birthday suit."

"Yeah, that makes two of us."

I headed to the bathroom. "Are you joining me?"

"Is that really a question?" He was out of bed with his hand on my hip within seconds. "That's an offer I'll never turn down."

***

My first time in Robert's office was one I wouldn't forget. Dressed in a floor-length ball gown—ruby red of course—I listened as Robert went through my instructions.

"Do you understand what you have to do, Allie?"

"Yes, Robert. I can handle it."

"There's still some time. Are you sure you don't want me to get someone from town hall in here?"

"No. It's not that I don't want to marry Levi, but I want to do it my way. I also refuse to deprive my mother of her right to be part of it. It's going to be hard enough to explain to her that her future grandchildren are going to have wings."

Helen laughed. I really was lucking out in the mother-in-law department.

Robert made complete eye contact. For once, it didn't intimidate me. "You are already bonded with Levi as his mate, but generally the queen is already married to the king."

"I want a summer wedding. I think after everything you can respect that wish."

Robert actually smiled. "I think I can. I also respect that you take your mother's feelings into consideration."

"My dad's too." I may not have said it, but I needed him there too.

"I promise I'll make her an honest woman this summer, Dad. We can't wait any longer for the coronation though." The wedding formality was for the human world, but it was important to the Laurent family too. More important than I expected.

"No, we can't wait. It's time for you to become king." Robert beamed at his son, and Levi looked equally happy. He may have downplayed it lately, but becoming King of The Society was huge to him.

"Have you two figured out what your retirement plans are?" I asked. Robert had been grilling me enough, it was his turn.

Helen smiled. "We're traveling. We haven't traveled on unofficial business for years."

Robert put an arm around Helen. He was so much more relaxed than usual. "This city is too small for us to stay around. It's Levi's turn to rule."

"Both of ours. Allie and I are doing this together." Levi squeezed my hand.

A knock on the door let us know that it was time.

"Let's do this," Levi whispered in my ear before he led me out on his arm.

The chambers were as cold as always, but I didn't mind it with Levi right next to me. We walked in behind Robert and Helen, and I held my head up high. I was about to become queen, it wasn't the time to get nervous. I looked around the room, grinning when I caught sight of Tiffany and Anne sitting in a middle row of stone seats. I smiled back when Toby gave me a thumbs up sign, and Cade winked. I looked all over for Hailey, and finally found her with Jared and Owen off to the side. I sighed with relief. Levi had listened to my one request.

Levi and I stood to the right of Robert and waited for him to begin.

"Welcome to this most important of occasions. After forty years, I am ready to hand over my crown to my son, Leviathan. He is ready to become your new king. His rule will only be enhanced by his queen, Allison. I assure you that I am leaving The Society in the finest of hands." Robert turned and took one of my hands, and one of Levi's.

Levi nodded and his father stepped back behind him. Helen kissed my cheek and did the same to Levi. I followed Levi's lead and kneeled. Robert placed his crown on Levi's head, and Helen removed my tiara and gave me her crown instead. The new headpiece was even heavier, but I didn't care. The reality of the situation hit me as Levi took my hand, and we stood up. I was a queen. I was the queen of a supernatural society.

Levi easily commanded the attention of the room. "Thank you all for being here today. We're glad you could witness this momentous occasion. Now, as is tradition, I will select my head of security and chief advisor."

"There's no one better prepared to assure to the security of the Laurent family and The Society than Jared Florence."

Jared shook Levi's hand before kissing me on the cheek and giving me a hug. "Glad we'll still get to spend time together, Allie."

I returned the hug, positive Levi had made the right decision. "I guess this means you can't call me princess anymore?"

"Officially, no, but I might slip accidently."

"That's all right. I might slip and call you a goon."

Levi leaned in to whisper. "If you two are done, I have another position to announce."

Jared grinned and faced forward.

Levi continued. "And Owen Kaye is the only one I'd trust as my advisor."

Owen and Levi shook hands before he hugged me. "Glad you guys worked everything out."

"Me too. Congratulations."

I looked out into the audience and found his parents. They looked like they might burst with excitement. This was big for them—huge.

Loud applause drowned out the conversation Levi had with his friends. I waited for the signal from Levi.

He took my hand before continuing. "Although tradition is important, sometimes it is just as important to embrace change—and create new traditions. Your queen has decided to take on an advisor of her own."

"I couldn't take on the position as queen without a trusted friend and advisor by my side. Hailey Kaye, will you accept the position?" Hailey meant more to me than I knew how to express in words. I needed to have her by my side as I moved into my new role.

"Yes!" She ran over and hugged me, eliciting laughter from the crowd. When we broke the hug, I saw Hailey's dad holding her mom. The pride on her face brought tears to my eyes.

Levi whispered in my ear. "All right, my queen, are you ready?"

"Of course. This is the easy part." He squeezed my hand before we left the room and headed upstairs to the reception.

Chapter Twenty-Two

Levi removed his hands from my eyes. "You can look now."

"The flamingo? You got me the flamingo?" I took two steps forward and ran my hand over the beautiful wood. He'd anchored it into the wall.

"Is it the right one?"

I felt the tears, and I didn't fight them. "Yes."

"Good." He put his arms around my waist, giving me just enough space that I could look at him.

"How'd you find it?"

"There weren't too many amusement parks that were selling off rides when you were seven."

"I can't believe you did this. It's unreal." I put a hand on his shoulder.

"It's very real. It's also sturdy. You can ride it if you want."

I laughed. "The only bird I'm riding is you."

He chuckled. "I love when you talk dirty."

"Yeah, well, you bring out that side in me."

"Right now I want to bring out another."

"Oh?"

"Do you know why I tracked down the flamingo?"

I leaned up to kiss him lightly. "Because you knew I wanted it, and you like to get me what I want."

He took my face in his hands. "It's a reminder."

"A reminder?" I leaned my head into his palm.

"That you will always come first. The Society, the crown, none of that matters as much as you do."

The tears started again—much heavier this time. "You'll always come first for me," I managed to choke out.

"Allie, my life is nothing without you. You are everything to me. Knowing I get to spend every day with you at my side as both my wife and queen makes everything we've been through worth it."

"I love you, Levi, and I love being your queen."

"We're going to be great together as long as we stop keeping secrets."

"I know." I smiled.

"Which is why it's time I reveal my last one."

"You have another secret?" I looked up into his blue-gray eyes.

"It's called an Oasis."

"What is?

"Your drink. It's rum, triple sec, and pineapple juice."

"You're finally revealing it?"

"I'm not worried about you leaving and finding the drink on your own."

"You're adorable." I leaned up to kiss him again.

"So are you." He really kissed me. It was sweet, intense, and everything I wanted. I could have kissed him forever, just standing there in the living room.

"If you're done admiring the flamingo, I'd love to get you back into bed."

"Will you carry me?"

"Anytime, love. Anytime."

I thought I was running away from life when I came to New Orleans that summer, but really I was running toward it. Sometimes you have to take flight to find your way home.

In the city that never sleeps, the chronicles continue. Follow the Pterons into the Empire Chronicles.

Soar (The Empire Chronicles #1) coming late 2013
http://www.alyssaroseivy.com/p/the-empire-chronicles.html

Keep reading for a preview of **The Hazards of Skinny Dipping**, a New Adult Romance by Alyssa Rose Ivy. For more information about Alyssa Rose Ivy's books, please visit her online at:

www.AlyssaRoseIvy.com
www.facebook.com/AlyssaRoseIvy
twitter.com/AlyssaRoseIvy
AlyssaRoseIvy@gmail.com

The Hazards of Skinny Dipping

By Alyssa Rose Ivy

Prologue

Skinny dipping was the last thing on my list. Of the five items, it was the hardest one for me. It wasn't a bucket list or anything like that—I wasn't thinking about death. It was a things-to-do-before-college list my cousin, Amy, made for me.

Now, I know what you're thinking. This is going to be one of those stories about the death of a loved one spurring a girl down a path of self-discovery. It's not. My cousin is alive and well, and at the time of this story was in Malawi with the Peace Corps. The list was her way of preparing me for the wilds of college (her words, not mine). Amy was under the impression that I was entirely unprepared for the life of a coed.

I still remember her exact words. We were hanging out in her room at her parents' house while she packed. "Juliet, sweetheart, you know I love you, right?"

I glanced at her apprehensively. "Yeah…"

"So know that, when I say this, it's out of love." She tossed a huge pile of t-shirts into her large black duffel.

I tensed. "Should I be scared?"

"No." She smiled her million-dollar, brings-guys-to-their-knees smile, and I knew I should actually be terrified.

"Okay." I clasped my hands together, refusing to look at my chipped nail polish.

She flipped long, dark hair off her shoulder. "I'm worried about you."

"Worried?"

"I don't want you to totally drown next year." She shoved a small, pink envelope into my hand. "Here, don't open this until after graduation."

"But you won't be here. You leave tomorrow."

She gave me her signature 'duh' look. "I'm well aware. Just open it, and do exactly what it says."

"This kind of feels like the beginning of a YA novel."

She laughed. "No. Trust me. The contents of this letter are not YA appropriate."

My stomach dropped. What was Amy getting me into?

I brought the envelope home and stared at it about four times a day for the next two weeks. Obviously, I could have just opened it, but I'm usually kind of a rules person. Each time I started to tear open the envelope, I chickened out. I kept picturing Amy's perfectly made up face yelling at me. I know that description doesn't quite fit with a girl who joined the Peace Corps, but if you knew Amy, you'd understand. She was just Miss Perfect. It wasn't until I got home from a graduation party at a friend's house that I finally opened it. As I unfolded the pale pink paper, a Georgia driver's license saying I was twenty-two fell into my lap. I set aside the fake ID and read the note.

Juliet's Must-Do Before College List

1) Get drunk (and no, a buzz from sugary drinks does not qualify as drunk).

2) Go to a bar. Any bar will do, but you need to at least know what they look like inside.

3) Wear something you know would give your father a heart attack if he saw it.

4) Kiss a random guy, and don't let it go further.

5) Go skinny dipping.

I'm sure you expect me to detail how I crossed the first four items off my list, but this story isn't about the first four. It's about what happened when I did number five.

Chapter One

Finally alone, I reveled in the silence, looking out the large floor-to-ceiling windows of my family's beach house. My grandparents had bought the house located just outside of Charleston, South Carolina years ago, before Kiawah became a retreat for millionaires. They were generous and let the entire extended family use it whenever we wanted. After two weeks of sharing the house with five other people, I was excited to have it to myself.

I'd decided to stay an extra day, craving some alone time before I had to give up all of my privacy and move in with some random girl. The whole idea of having a roommate sounded good in theory, but knowing my luck, I'd be living with my exact opposite or something even worse.

Sitting cross-legged on the ultra-comfy bed (now that everyone had left, I had moved up from the pull-out couch), I took the now crinkled letter out of my green REI backpack. Go skinny dipping. If I was ever going to do it, an empty beach house was the perfect place. Besides, I was running out of time. School started in just a few weeks.

It was already after nine, and the last remnants of the sun had disappeared. I picked out my favorite red bikini and changed. I'd have to ease into the whole thing, maybe jump in the pool and then take it off. It's funny that getting drunk and kissing a random guy didn't scare me, but getting naked in a pool seemed terrifying. I just wasn't comfortable being naked. I knew my body wasn't bad. I was decently thin with curves in all the right places—namely my chest. The few guys I'd been with always seemed happy enough with my body, but I still didn't like shedding my clothes. I know some girls walk around their rooms naked. Not me. I was dried off and in clothes within minutes of getting out of the shower. Okay, that's not entirely true. I loved sitting around in a towel, but you had to be careful doing that when you lived in a house with a couple of brothers.

I changed into my bikini and headed outside. One side of the house bordered the woods, and the house on the other side had been empty for the two weeks I'd been at the beach. I knew that well. I'd been disappointed when the Bradleys failed to show up.

Something was still missing. If I was going skinny dipping, I was going to do it right. I went back inside to get my iPod. I plugged it into the outside stereo system and selected my workout list. I needed something upbeat.

Satisfied with the musical selection, I jumped in. I wasn't good with the whole easing myself in slowly thing. It was too cold that way.

It was only after I'd jumped in that I realized I'd forgotten one important thing—a towel. I thought about getting out for one, but then I'd get cold. There was no sense going through it twice.

I dove under the surface and tried to make myself relax. It wasn't a big deal. I needed to pretend it was a bath—a big, outside bath. I pulled the elastic out of my hair, letting my long, light brown hair fall down my back. My mom called my hair dirty blonde, but I hated anything with the name dirty. It was light brown.

I finally made myself do it. I untied my top and slipped off the bottoms. Oh my god, I'd done it. I was actually naked. I flung both pieces to the side, trying to get them to land on one of the lounge chairs, but somehow they ended up on the decking underneath. It didn't really matter since I wouldn't be putting them back on. I'd just run up to my room and change.

Amy hadn't specified how long I needed to skinny dip, but I figured I needed to at least swim around a little. The more I did it, the less weird it seemed. It felt liberating. The water was warm enough, and with only a few lights illuminating the pool, I didn't feel overly exposed.

That excitement lasted maybe another five minutes until I saw headlights pull into the neighbor's driveway. Unfortunately, they had one of those windy driveways that curved around to a garage in back. If the driver happened to look through the trees and shrubs, I'd be spotted. Before I panicked, I reassured myself that it was too dark for anyone to actually see anything.

I didn't have much time to worry. The car stopped, and a tall figure stepped out.

"Hey, is that you, Juliet?" It may have been dark, but I'd know that voice anywhere. It was deep and incredibly sexy.

I wanted to slip under the water and never come back up. Dylan Bradley was talking to me while I was naked. "Uh, yeah. Hi, Dylan." To this day, I blame it on the music. If Katy Perry hadn't been blaring, he might never have looked.

"Isn't it a little late for a swim?"

"Not really. I like staying up late." Could I sound lamer?

He disappeared, but I knew it wasn't over. He reappeared a moment later through a patch of trees.

I treaded water in the deepest part of the pool, hoping the dim lighting hid how completely naked I was.

"Mind if I turn that down?" He pointed up at the speakers.

"Sure. The controls are—"

"Behind the bar. I know." Dylan had spent plenty of nights swimming at our house. Even though his house was far bigger, his dad had refused to put in a pool. Mr. Bradley claimed that if you were at the beach, you didn't need a manmade concrete hole to swim in.

Dylan turned off the music. So much for turning it down. "I heard you're going to Harrison this year."

"Yeah. I'm actually starting college." I continued treading water, praying he wouldn't move any closer.

"Cool. I'll probably see you around then."

"Oh yeah, I forgot you were still up there." Total lie. I was well aware Dylan was a senior at Harrison University. I hated to admit it, but I Facebook stalked him. I'd probably have real life stalked him if we didn't live five hours away from each other. To say I had a crush on Dylan would be the understatement of the century.

His expression let me know how little he believed me. "Yeah. It's my last year, but Kyle's going to be a freshman."

"Yeah?" I, of course, knew that too, but not from internet stalking. I couldn't care less about his brother, Kyle. It was Dylan who always had my attention. I'd found out about Kyle's plans from my mother.

Dylan looked even better than I remembered. Despite the dim lighting, I could see his slight tan—normally it was a lot deeper. I guess his summer internship had kept him from spending as much time at the beach as usual. His brown hair still had just a little bit of a curl to it. He wore it shorter than I'd ever remembered seeing it.

"You look kind of cold. Where's your towel?" He glanced around.

"Oh, I'm okay."

"Come on, you can't stay in the pool all night."

I would stay as long as I had to.

"Wait a second." A small smile spread across his face. He walked toward the chairs, and my heart sunk. When he turned back toward me, he had my bikini top wrapped around his hand. "Are you skinny dipping?"

"Umm, maybe."

"By yourself?"

What was that supposed to mean? "Isn't that part obvious?"

He grinned. "Wow, I never took you for an exhibitionist."

"This is a private pool."

"Now you really need to get out."

"Shut up. Not until you leave."

"You're too cold. You won't make it that long."

"You're wrong." I sure hoped he was.

"All right. If you're not getting out anytime soon, I'm going to join you." He pulled off his t-shirt.

Oh my god. Was Dylan Bradley about to get naked in front of me? I had to be dreaming. This was not the kind of thing that ever happened to me—at least not when I was awake.

I was so busy freaking out that I didn't even try to stop him. The next thing I knew, he stood buck naked in front of me. I admired the view in shock for a second before he jumped in. He swam over to me, but held back. "You're eighteen, right?"

"Yeah. Why does that matter?"

He smiled. "Because I'm not getting busted for swimming naked with a minor."

"It's stupid, isn't it? I mean it's not like I magically changed from a kid to an adult on my last birthday." I stupidly used hand motions and unwittingly gave Dylan a front row view of my breasts.

His eyes widened. "You haven't been a kid for a while."

"Yeah, you either." I cringed. I really needed to filter.

He laughed. "No, no I haven't."

The way he stared unnerved me, and I needed to keep us talking. "What are you doing here? School starts in like two weeks. Isn't this a weird time to come to the beach?"

"I've been working all summer. It's the only break I've had."

I really looked at him. To be honest, he did look tired, although it was hard to look at his face when I knew he wasn't wearing anything.

He suddenly grinned. "You're going to be such trouble."

"Excuse me?"

"I figured you'd spend all of your time in the library, but now that I know about this side of you, I have a feeling you're going to make things interesting."

"You make it sound like we're going to be hanging out."

"We're not?" He moved into the shallow water.

"Do you usually hang out with freshman girls?"

"Sometimes." He leaned back against the wall. I didn't need the show he was giving me. He definitely felt comfortable in his own skin.

"I'm not going to bite, Juliet. You can come over here. You can't tread water all night."

"Not all night, but for a while. I was on the swim team, and I'm a lifeguard."

"Come on, don't be a baby."

I shouldn't have let his words get to me, but they did. I let out a breath and swam over. "Who are you calling a baby?" Of course, I was on my knees to keep myself under the water.

"Not you. I'm definitely not calling you that." He pulled on my hand, catapulting me through the water and against him. He slid down, so that I was practically on his lap. Oh my god. If being naked with him was scary, having the evidence of his arousal pressed against me was unreal.

I tried to move off him, but all that did was shift me closer.

"You're gorgeous."

I'm sure I blushed. "Oh, thanks."

"I mean it. I've thought so for a while, but you always seemed so young."

"Yeah? I thought that about you, too."

"The gorgeous part or the young part?"

"Neither. I mean. I just mean I always thought you were attractive."

He smiled. "I know."

"You know?"

"I assumed that's why you always put on the tiniest bikinis and lay out right in front of us. Unless that was for Kyle's benefit…"

"No. It was for yours." My wardrobe and schedule had always been strategically planned to result in the maximum amount of exposure to Dylan. I was pathetic. I'm not even going to try to deny it.

He grinned. "I knew it."

He ran his hands up and down my arms. "You've got goose bumps."

"That's the problem with the shallow end. Not enough of you is under water."

"Want me to fix that?"

"How?"

He didn't answer. Instead, he gripped my hand and swam back to the deep end, stopping to anchor himself on the ladder. "Is this better?" He never released me, but kept me tethered to him so I couldn't swim away.

"Much." I was proud of myself for not hyperventilating.

"Good." He pulled me against him. "Maybe this will keep you warm, too."

"Umm, yeah."

"Am I making you nervous?"

"No," I lied.

"Are you a virgin?" He suddenly got serious.

"No, of course not."

"I figured you weren't."

"Because I look like a slut or something?"

"No. But you're hot, and you've had boyfriends here with you before."

"Okay, good." For some reason, even though I was naked in a pool with him, I was still worried about Dylan's opinion about the kind of girl I was.

"Would it be okay if I kissed you?"

We were currently naked together, with me on his lap, and now he was asking my permission to kiss me? I nodded.

"Good." He leaned in, cradling the back of my head as his lips met mine. His lips moved, slowly for a moment, before he sped up and pushed his way into my mouth. He deepened the kiss while using his free hand to cup one of my breasts. I groaned. That seemed to turn him on more, and his kiss became frenzied. His hand left my breast and slipped between my legs. I'd wondered what those fingers would feel like, and they didn't disappoint. His lips left mine and moved down to my neck. He stopped. "Touch me."

After a moment's hesitation, I reached out to grab him.

"My house or yours?"

It took me a moment to pull out of my fog and realize what he was asking.

His hand stilled. "I mean we could do it here, but I figure you want to use protection."

"Oh, yeah. Of course. Yours." There was no way I was doing it in my grandparents' house. But oh my god, I was about to have sex with Dylan.

"Great." He didn't waste a minute. He got us out of the pool, picked up his jeans, and towed me to his house. He moved so quickly I didn't have time to worry about how naked I was. He pulled out his keys and hurriedly unlocked his back door.

"Aren't we going to get everything wet?"

"Oh, we're going to get things wet."

"I meant the house. Because of the pool."

"I know what you meant." He pushed open the door to his room and backed me up to the bed. He leaned over me until I lay down.

I looked up at him, wondering if this was actually happening.

"I'm really glad I came down to the beach." He hovered over me, kissing my neck while his hand moved between my legs again. "Are you ready for me, Juliet?"

"Yes," I managed to squeak.

"Don't move." He got off the bed.

I sat up. What the hell was happening?

He returned a minute later. I couldn't help gawking at his naked body. He was all muscle—but not in the overly built-up way.

"I told you not to move."

"Where'd you go?"

"I knew Kyle kept a stash here. I think he was waiting for a chance to use one with you." With that charming statement, Dylan opened a condom. "It looks like he's out of luck." He moved above me with a grin on his face. "I got to you first."

I don't know what I expected, but this wasn't it. I winced when he entered me. It had been a while. I waited for the fireworks to start, but none did, and I mean none. There was absolutely nothing special or noteworthy about it—it was just sex—and incredibly unsatisfying sex at that.

What felt like thirty seconds later, he rolled off of me. "Fucking amazing."

Amazing? Did we experience the same thing? But this was Dylan Bradley. Clearly, the problem was with me. "Yeah, definitely."

"I'm so glad you're going to Harrison. This is going to be a fun year."

Was he implying this was more than a one-time thing? Did he want to actually date me? Of course, that was something I should have thought about before hooking up, but I was willing to break my no random sex rule for Dylan.

"No one's expecting you home, right?"

"No. I already called my parents tonight."

"Good." He pulled me close.

"Do you want me to stay?"

"Of course." He didn't say anything else, and less than a minute later, he was sleeping.

What the hell?

I pushed against his arm. The last thing I was ready to do was sleep. After a couple of attempts, I was able to move his arm enough to slip out. I looked down at the ground, remembering I had one slight problem—no clothes. I decided to escape to the bathroom. It took my eyes a few seconds to adjust once I turned on the light. I stared at my reflection in the mirror—my hair was a wet mess, and my neck and cheeks were red from his stubble.

I opened the closet and thankfully found a towel. It was plush and blue and suited my purposes perfectly. I stopped by the bed to look at Dylan for a second before heading out the back door. I wondered what he'd think when he woke up, and I wasn't there. Most likely, he wouldn't care. I walked back to our house still wearing just the towel and poured myself a glass of water. I took a shower and pulled on my favorite light green pajamas before finally collapsing into bed.

I stared at the ceiling for a while. It wasn't Dylan's fault it had been so disappointing. It had probably been because I'd inflated him so much. He was just a guy. Hopefully, it would be better next time—if there was a next time. I was almost positive this wasn't what Amy had in mind, but skinny dipping before college may have been a good thing—or so I thought.

The Hazards of Skinny Dipping is available now!